**The man was rising slowly
with his gun out ...**

Longarm could read the killing intentions of that towering bastard, but for some fool reason, his own gun hand barely seemed to be moving through the glue-thick air.

Some son of a bitch seemed to have poured melted tar in his damn holster, judging from the way his .44 was coming out, too slow to save him, as that red-eyed rascal's gun muzzle trained on him again.

Then in the same dreamy, slow way, the side of the gunslick's head evaporated in a big, frothy cloud of strawberry jam.

A hollow voice boomed, "Custis, are you hurt?"

He looked up at Tess to answer weakly, "Nope, but I reckon I'm poisoned again ..."

TABOR EVANS

LONGARM

AND THE BIG SHOOT-OUT

A JOVE BOOK

LONGARM AND THE BIG SHOOT-OUT

A Jove Book/published by arrangement with
the author

PRINTING HISTORY
Jove edition/January 1986

ISBN: 0-515-08445-X

Jove books are published by The Berkley Publishing Group,
200 Madison Avenue, New York, N.Y. 10016.
The words "A JOVE BOOK" and the "J" with sunburst
are trademarks belonging to Jove Publications, Inc.

PRINTED IN THE UNITED STATES OF AMERICA

Chapter 1

The Parthenon Saloon was too respectable to let customers in skirts belly up to the bar, so Longarm knew
where to look when Sergeant Nolan of the Denver police
informed him that a lady desired his company in one of
the side rooms, where a female customer could get drunk
discreetly.

The first thing Longarm noted as he joined the vapidly
pretty sort of buck-toothed blonde who had sent for him
was that "lady" had been putting it a mite strong. For,
when last they'd met, in the tough little mining camp of
Creed, Miss Chipmunk Alice had been selling her body
three ways for two dollars, and some said she cut her
prices on off nights.

Longarm removed his Stetson as he sat down across
the tiny table from her, but he didn't ask her permission
to smoke. The little private room was sort of stuffy to
begin with, and Chipmunk Alice looked sick enough
already. She wasn't wearing her usual whore paint, and
her dark blue duds looked almost respectable. He was
too polite to ask the soiled dove whether she was re-

formed or dying. He assumed she would tell him in her own good time.

The ashen-faced Alice poured an unsteady tumbler of rye from the bottle she had bought and announced, "They only brought me this one glass, Custis, but we can share it if you ain't too proud."

He repressed a grimace of distaste. "That's all right, Miss Alice," he told her. "I just inhaled the free lunch they serve out front and washed it down with two schooners of needled beer. So I'd best pass on your kind offer. I'm still on duty this afternoon and, while we're on the subject, they only give me an hour off for lunch."

She sighed and had the drink all to herself, neat. Then she poured another as she asked him, "Do you mind the time I gave you that tip on the Muller Brothers and you said you owed me, Custis?"

He nodded soberly. "I do. But I'm still on my lunch hour. I got to get back to my office. So let's get down to brass tacks, Miss Alice."

"You're only going to laugh at me, like everyone else. I know it sounds silly—even to me—but, damn it, don't a girl like me have *any* rights?"

"You look free, white, and, no offense, well over twenty-one. So, if it's in the Constitution, you got it. What in thunder are we talking about, Miss Alice?"

She sniffed and said, "I'm getting raped. I mean regular, not just once. When I took him to the law up in Creed, they just laughed at me mean. I moved to Leadville to get away from the brute and, when he raped me some more there, the Leadville law told me not to be silly. But, durn it, Custis, I'm pure sick and tired of being raped, and *somebody* has to make him stop!"

Longarm didn't answer. It was hard to talk and keep a straight face as the poor little critter stared at him like

2

that. She sobbed, "I knew you'd just laugh, like all the others. You don't think it could be called rape, either, do you?"

He shrugged and observed, "At the very least one could call it theft of services, Miss Alice. Are you saying one gent in particular has been pestering your person without offering to pay?"

She nodded grimly. "His name is Buckskin Billy Bancroft and, though he says I'm his one true love, he's just mean as hell and I got bruises to prove it. Would you like to see my bruises, Custis?"

Longarm shook his head and said, "Not hardly. I'll take your word this jasper's been acting mighty odd, Miss Alice. What was that about your being his true love . . . no offense?"

"He paid me the first time," she said. "He said he'd just got outten State Prison and hadn't had a woman for years. So I done my best to make it up to him, even though he needed a bath and come to bed with his spurs on. I reckon I may have overdone it, for the next time he come back he said I was the girl of his dreams and that he aimed to reform me. That's what Buckskin Billy calls slapping a girl silly and taking her for free . . . reforming. Like I said, I run away from him to Leadville, but he caught up with me there and gave me a fat lip as well as a screwing that just ruint me for the evening. Now he's followed me to Denver, and I don't know what I'm to do."

Longarm frowned thoughtfully. "Did he mention how come he got so hard up in State Prison, Miss Alice?"

The whore said, "Manslaughter. He kilt a cowhand in Jimtown over a dance-hall gal. He said he was searching for her some more when he discovered I was an even better lay, and that now that he's found his dream girl

3

I'll never get away from him."

Longarm took out his watch to consult it. He was already late getting back to the office. Chipmunk Alice had another stiff belt and asked wistfully, "Won't you arrest him for me, Custis?"

Longarm sighed. "I'd like to, but I can't. Rape ain't a federal offense, even if you was a schoolmarm, off a government reservation. If you was an Indian, or even a military dependent, I could arrest the hell out of him for you. But the fair city of Denver would frown on my butting into their jurisdiction."

"What are you thinking, Custis Long?" Asked Chipmunk Alice as the tall federal deputy's gun-metal eyes stared through her at some other picture. "I know that hunting look of old, you sweet man! You're aiming to just gun him for me, right?"

Longarm shook his head soberly. "Too much paperwork, smack in the middle of such a big sissy town. But I drink regular with some local copper badges, and there's more'n one way to skin a cat or put a lovesick lunatic out of business. So let's study on this dumb situation."

She brightened and asked, "Are we talking about that nice-looking police officer who asked me so polite what I wanted, just a while ago?"

Longarm nodded, but said, "Never mind how nice-looking Sergeant Nolan might be. His wife is a sweet little gal. You say you know where this Buckskin Billy can be found right now?"

She gave him the address of a rooming house out along Broadway. He tore a leaf out of his notebook and wrote it down before he went on to tell her, "The first thing we have to change is your story. No matter who asks, Buckskin Billy's never once enjoyed your charms in full, see?"

4

"Custis, that's just not true. The brute's had it in me all three ways, against my expressed desires and at the cost of considerable discomfort on my part, I don't mind telling you!"

"Don't tell anyone else, then, for rape is a hard charge to prove, even when the victim *is* a schoolmarm, which you ain't."

"I know it," she sobbed. "You men are all alike, you brutes!"

He nodded and soothed, "That's what I just said. You see, us brutes have all found ourselves confused and mayhaps wrestling on a porch swing with some silly gal whose earlier signals we must have read wrong. You just need one man on the jury who's had a gal say no when he thought she meant yes, and there goes your case."

"Then how can a ravaged woman hope to convince you brutes when she really means no, damn it?"

"I said it wasn't easy, even for a gal with a better rep. But while all too many men can see themselves in a situation where a teasing gal got them a mite overexcited, there's one thing no man born of mortal woman could see himself doing. So that's what we'd best tell Nolan. Ain't it disgusting that poor Buckskin Billy makes a habit of *exposing* himself to women like that?"

"Exposing? You mean just taking it out and waving it about?"

"Yep. He must have gone loco, jerking off in State Prison all those years. Who but a maniac would want to act so silly? I know *I* sure as hell can't see myself exposing my private parts to a full dressed woman in broad day, no matter *who* she might be! So that's what he's been doing around you of late, and you have every right to feel chagrined, Miss Alice."

She started to object, then laughed uncertainly and

asked, "Do you think they'd believe such a crazy tale? He's certain to deny it, and it would be just my word against his, right?"

Longarm shook his head and said, "Wrong. In the first place, you won't be called on to testify about such disgusting matters if you hop the next train back to the high country. In the second place, the copper badges are used to hearing all sorts of excuses from such pathetic critters. Exposure ain't a serious enough breach of the peace to bind anyone over to the grand jury, but it sure can be embarrassing as hell to explain in front of the streetwalkers and vagrants lined up in night court."

The pallid whore frowned and told him, "I know all about night court. They can't give him more than a few months without a full jury trial. Damn it, Custis, he *hurt* me!"

"I know. If he ever comes near you again, you just repeat the same story, and they'll give him another fifty days or fifty dollars, Miss Alice. I doubt he will. I know *I'd* sure be disgusted with a gal who accused me of such idiotic behavior even once."

She laughed again, but asked, "Do you reckon they'd believe a girl like me, even up in Creed where they know for a fact what I am?"

He said, "Sure they would. Why on earth would anyone make up such a silly charge? It's an article of male faith that mean-hearted women accuse men of rape when they're just out to get an innocent gent in trouble." He got to his feet as he added, "It's also well known among real he-men that anyone accused of self-exposure has to have been doing *something* peculiar. So you'd best head for the depot and leave the rest to me, Miss Alice."

She smiled gratefully up at him. "My train won't leave for a spell, and the lock on that door looks solid. The

6

least I can offer by way of thanks is . . . well, you know . . ."

He smiled down gallantly and expressed his regret that he had to get back to the office, pronto. So she gave him a raincheck on her kind offer, and he left.

He knew there wasn't time, damn it, but he still went back out to the bar, bought Nolan a beer, and explained the situation as it now looked to him, adding, "The little gal is too flusterpated to press charges, personal, Sarge. But I thought it my civic duty to tell you there was a dicky-waver on your beat. I got the address here if you want it."

The burly police sergeant wrinkled his nose in disgust as he took the slip of paper, scanned it, and growled, "That's not too far from the Evans Grammar School. And you say he just whips it out and stands there drooling?"

"That's what the gal says, Nolan. I asked her if he actually laid hands on her, but she says he just jerked off at her, saying something dumb about her being his true love."

"Oh, shit, we'd better round him up before school lets out this afternoon! He could scare those little girls at Evans out of a year's growth. You say that *grown* gal who told you about him refuses to press charges?"

"She got red as a beet just whispering her tale to me, and I know her personally. I tried to get her to make it a more serious attempt on her virtue, but she says she's too embarrassed."

"I don't blame her. She wasn't bad-looking. A man would have to be loco to whip it out in such fine company and then just stand there jerking off. Leave the poor sick bastard to us, Longarm. Mayhaps after he falls down the stairs a few times he'll learn to act more sensible around some folks."

7

They shook on it and parted friendly. The Parthenon was close to the federal building, and Longarm was a fast walker even when a crisp spring breeze wasn't blowing down off the Front Range. But he was still late as hell, even for him, and so as he entered the rear office of his superior, Chief Marshal Billy Vail, he found his short stocky boss in a red-faced snit. Vail rose behind his desk to point at the banjo clock on the oak-paneled wall and roar, "I don't want to hear your excuses! I don't care if you just stopped the James boys from robbing the bank across the street, you lazy good-for-nothing rascal! Where the hell have you been all this time?"

Longarm took a seat in the leather chair across the desk from Vail and reached for a smoke as he replied demurely, "I wish you'd make up your mind, boss. First you tell me you don't care why I got back so late, and then you ask my why. Well, it all started up in Creed, a year or more ago. You sent me up to find the Muller Brothers, and—"

"Shut up!" snapped Vail, dropping into his swivel chair. "Luckily for you, the train you have to catch don't leave for another two hours. If you miss it, you can commend your soul to Jesus, for your ass shall be reamed by me! I have your travel orders already typed up here somewhere."

Longarm didn't answer as he lit his three-for-a-nickel cheroot. Vail found the onionskins he was looking for and handed them over, growling, "I'm sending you east to Tangleroost, Arkansas. You can pick up a mount when you get there, but you'd best take along your Winchester and plenty of ammo, for the area's a mite wild and it lies betwixt Younger's Bend and Clay County, Missouri. Need I say more?"

Longarm blew a thoughtful smoke ring and said,

"You'd better. If you think the James–Younger gang is anywhere near their old home grounds this late in the game, you'd best have your head examined, Billy. Poor old Belle Starr can hardly use her shithouse these days without some Pinkerton dick wiping her ass, and the Pinks have the old James homestead in Clay County so staked out that Mother James is said to be training beans up their fool legs this spring. I know you're mad at me, but do I have to go on another wild-goose chase just because I got back a mite late from lunch?"

Vail smiled despite himself. "Wild geese is just about the size of it," he admitted. "But we ain't discussing the James–Younger gang right now. *Real* wild geese, the kind with wings, will be coming up that flyway any minute now. Marshal Moran, over that way, is an old pal of mine. We rode together in the Rangers under Big Foot Johnson. So when he sent out a call for help I had to tell him I could at least spare you. You'll be working sort of under cover. Moran's own deputies are sort of famous around Tangleroost. So he wants extra hands the locals might have more trouble making out as the law."

Longarm shrugged and said, "At least I can dress more sensible if I ain't on duty official. Who's your old pal after, Billy?"

Vail frowned thoughtfully. "Anyone whose handsome visage might appear on recent federal wants, of course. The big shootoff's likely to attract all sorts of gunslicks. Easy-sounding money often does, you know."

Longarm consulted his mental railroad map for a few more drags on his cheroot. He shook his head and said, "I know where the township of Tangleroost is, now. It don't have much to recommend it as a source of easy money, boss. Last time I passed through, it was a jerk-water stop in a big soggy stretch of flood-killed timber

9

along the lower Arkansas, on the dumb side of the natural levee."

Vail nodded. "I know. It's mostly oxbow lakes and dead standing timber, like you said. There's only the one settlement where the trains stop for water, crossing that stretch of undrained deltaland. That's where you'll be reporting to Marshal Moran. He'll give you further instructions."

"On what, God damn it?" Longarm insisted. "Billy, there ain't anything worth stealing in that forsaken little swamp town. So why in thunder should all these wanted gunslicks descend on it all at once, to do what?"

Vail leaned back to light an even stinkier smoke before he said, "I told you. The great spring bird migration is fixing to commence in earnest, and they call that flooded stretch the Tangleroost because all sorts of birds find that tangle a mighty attractive roosting place. Between all that timber and standing water, all but deserted by humankind, that big swamp attracts birds from woodpeckers to whooping cranes. Before Armour and Swift larnt to ship better preserved beef east, cheaper, the market hunters had a happy hunting ground indeed in the Tangleroost."

Longarm said, "I know that. But there ain't much money in market hunting these days and, even when there was, not too many wanted outlaws were attracted to the trade. Market hunting is hard work. It ain't just the shooting. Pitchforking dead ducks into pickle barrels can get tedious as hell. So why does Marshal Moran expect a mess of lazy crooks to go fowling for a living, when it's so much more profitable to steal cows?"

Vail said, "This time there's over ten thousand dollars in prize money up for grabs by the best shot of the day. The Amalgamated Ammunition Trust is holding a big

10

shootoff in the Tangleroost this spring. Ten days' shooting, with a thousand dollars in cash going to the marks-
man who rings down the biggest bag of each day."

Longarm grimaced. "That sounds just plain disgusting. Have you any notion how many birds one man can
bag in a day with a punt gun, Billy? If even a dozen
contestants get to blazing at them poor dumb birds all at
once—"

"I know," Vail cut in. "The Smithsonian is sending
out some bird watchers to count the carnage, too. They've
asked the government to call off the contest as a crime
against nature. So that's something else for Moran and
the rest of you to worry about. There ain't no federal
law against shooting wild game over private land, and
the ammo company's leased the whole township for the
fool contest. The dudes from the Smithsonian figure to
make almost as much noise as the whooping cranes, and
you know how rustic some old country boys can act
around dudes who ain't even pestering 'em."

Longarm blew smoke out of his nostrils and moaned,
"Oh, Lord! Dead ducks falling on my head and sissy
dudes yelling in my ears about it all at once! Can't you
find me a nicer chore, like cleaning out cesspools, Billy?
I swear I'll skip lunch all next week if you'll only send
someone else. Just thinking about a whole swamp full
of rotting poultry has ruined my appetite entire!"

But Vail said, "You have your orders. Oh, I almost
forgot. Moran wants you to pick up one of them Smithsonian bird watchers as you pass through Kansas as well.
His name's Winslow. He's been banding sage hens around
Dodge City, for some fool reason, and now the Smithsonian wants him to join their other bird watchers around
Tangleroost. Moran figures he'll be safer riding in with
you."

Longarm smiled thinly and replied, "I don't see why. He must be pretty tough if he's been watching birds around Dodge and nobody's shot his toes off yet. But, all right, where do I find this fool nature lover?"

Vail handed over another flimsy. "Alhambra Hotel. And don't rawhide the poor dude. I mean it."

Longarm put the address away. "I hardly ever pick on sissies. Maybe he can explain what the hell's going on further east. I know nothing I've heard so far makes a lick of sense."

Chapter 2

Later that afternoon, as Longarm was stocking up on smokes and reading material at the Union Depot, a familiar voice hailed him and he turned to see Crawford of the *Post* approaching the same newsstand in the waiting room. The reporter said, "I figured to find you here. Heard you were going to the big shootoff in the Arkansas delta country."

Longarm looked disgusted. "It was supposed to be undercover. Never mind who told you. What can you tell me about this Amalgamated Ammunition Trust? I never heard of the rascals. What's wrong with Remington or Savage ammo? You don't see *them* ordering the execution of poor dumb ducks, do you?"

Crawford laughed. "That's because they're household words," he said. "A new outfit needs publicity to get its brand well known. They're listed with the stock exchange, if that's what you want to know. Were you suspecting them of something, Longarm?"

The taller lawman shrugged. "I reckon there's no law against simple stupidity," he said. "I got to check my luggage now."

The reporter tagged along as Longarm toted his

possibles and cased Winchester over to the baggage-checking counter. Longarm failed to see why. He really didn't know anything the reporter didn't. Crawford could see it was up to him to keep the conversation going, so he said, "I just come from the police station. Things are dull all over today, it seems. All they had for me on the blotter was a degenerate they picked up near a grammar school, and my editor won't want to print *that*."

Longarm slid his gear across the counter and got his claim check. "How come?" he asked, more cheerfully. "Don't you reckon it's the duty of the *Post* to warn parents about such rascals on or about school grounds?"

Crawford shook his head. "This particular dicky waver won't be bothering any kids for a spell. After he somehow managed to fall down seven or eight flights of stairs in a three-story boarding house, he made the mistake of charging old Sergeant Nolan with police brutality. So Judge Jenkins added resisting arrest and rape as an afterthought."

Longarm whistled softly. "Do tell? Who did they find to press such serious charges against the rascal?"

"Nobody," Crawford said. "He confessed of his own free will. He seemed mighty upset to be charged with self-exposure, so he got to bragging right in court that he was no such sissy. He said he was a real he-man. Then he asked them to hunt up some whore he raped regular so she could back him up. Judge Jenkins said that was silly, but as long as he wanted to stand trial as a self-confessed rapist the state of Colorado would be only too happy to oblige him. The Denver police bound him over to the state, and he'll get his expressed desires, soon as he gets out of the hospital. Like I said, it's too disgusting a story to print. How come you're grinning like that, Longarm?"

The tall deputy said it was because it looked as if his train would leave on time for a change, and legged out to the platform too fast for anyone to follow without a good reason. Crawford didn't bother.

Actually, the train didn't leave for another six or seven minutes. Longarm was seated comfortably by a coach window, reading the *Police Gazette*, when the train suddenly started with a jerk and a hundred and twenty odd pounds of soft brunette sat on his lap instead of the plush seat at his side she'd likely been aiming at. She gasped as if she'd sat on a tack and slid swiftly off, saying, "Oh, I beg your pardon, sir! Whatever must you think of me?"

Longarm smiled at her. "I think the train jolted your limbs out from under you unexpectedly, ma'am," he said. "But, as you can see, we've both survived the awesome railroad accident, so let's say no more about it."

She dimpled and replied, "Oh, dear, I've ruined the paper you were reading, haven't I?"

Longarm couldn't deny that. The *Police Gazette* was now a pink ruin, and the lady in tights on the cover would never be the same even if he pasted her together again. "I may be able to buy you another when the candy butcher comes through this car," she said.

He laughed and told her she looked too young to buy the *Police Gazette*. She either was, or was more likely just too dumb to know what he meant. She said, "I insist. It's the least I can do. My name is Penny Twinkles, Mr...?"

"Long. Custis Long. You must be an actress, right?"

"As a matter of fact I'm a dancer. How did you know?"

"Lucky guess, I reckon. You're too pretty to be a milkmaid, Miss Twinkles."

"Oh, dear, do you think this outfit is too gaudy, Mr. Long? I wouldn't want anyone to think I'm a... well, a dance-hall dancer! I only dance on the legitimate stage."

He studied her traveling duds judiciously, since she'd invited him to. She was dressed sedately enough in a pin-striped suit and a ridiculous straw hat. The boater pinned to her upswept and likely dyed black hair wouldn't have looked so stupid if it hadn't had a dead hummingbird pinned to it. He told her she looked prim and proper enough. Lots of gals seemed to fancy dead birds on their hats. He didn't know why. But lots of female notions made no sense when you studied on them. He folded up the tattered remains of his ruined *Gazette* and stuffed them down between the armrest and the windowsill. Across the aisle an old gal with a pickled-up mouth and eyes like stewed prunes was watching them both, mean as hell. Longarm understood *her* female notions well enough. The poor old critter likely suspected him of evil thoughts about the younger and much prettier gal who'd had the good taste to pick a seat beside him. He hoped when *he* got too old to enjoy the opposite sex he wouldn't hold it against the whole world so obviously.

He asked the little dancer where she was headed and she said back East, explaining, "I have to change trains at Pueblo."

He said it was a small world and that he would be proud to help her with her luggage in Pueblo, since they would both be riding the same eastbound together. The old bat across the aisle looked like she wanted to come over and bite him on the leg. He told the much nicer one beside him, "There's just time for an early supper before we reach Pueblo, if we run forward now and grab a table ahead of the stampede, Miss Twinkles."

She said that sounded like a grand idea and added that he could call her Penny if he would answer to Custis. He said it was a small sacrifice to make, so they got up

16

and headed for the dining car.

For a gal who said she danced for a living, Penny Twinkles sure needed to be helped a lot aboard a moving train. But she was a good sport about it and didn't say anything the few times he had to grab her sort of indelicately to keep her from falling down.

The dining car was still closed when they finally got to it, or it would have been had not the waiter who answered Longarm's knocks remembered him fondly of old. As he led them to a table in the otherwise empty diner, Penny said, "Oh, you must be someone *important,* Custis. Do you work for the railroad?"

He said, "Not exactly. I ride this line a lot on business."

It wasn't exactly a lie, and Billy Vail had told him he'd be working under cover once he left Denver. He was glad, just the same, that he still had on the fool tweed suit and shoestring tie they made him wear around the federal building. Penny might not have sat down so hard on a gent dressed cow.

She didn't ask him what sort of business he was in. She seemed more interested in talking about herself. Longarm listened politely and didn't comment when she went on and on about how poorly her exotic dancing had been received out West. That was what she called what she did—exotic dancing. He had already noticed that her curvaceous torso seemed more suited to bumps and grinds than the old soft shoe.

He didn't care how she danced. Dancing with her wasn't what he had in mind. When she asked if he thought she could get a Pullman bed out of Pueblo he assured her he knew that train crew personally, too, and held back on suggesting that a private compartment for the two of them might be even nicer. He would be getting

17

off a lot sooner, he knew, and he had to study her some before he bit off more than he might want to chew. She was pretty as hell, and by now he felt sure she hadn't really given him that free sample of her rump by accident. But there was more to romance than soft rumps.

Penny talked too much for a gal with so little to say. When the waiter brought their before-dinner drinks and she sent hers back because it wasn't made right, Longarm began to suspect he knew why she was traveling alone. A gal had to be more than pretty to make up for being a tedious dimwit with fancy airs. The romance really began to go sour when the first course was served and she sniffed at it and opined she was used to fancier grub than she'd found anywhere west of the Big Muddy so far. Longarm just dug in. He doubted she would like to hear about all the times he had eaten worse, or not at all.

By dessert she had caught on, and told him the apple pie wasn't half bad. That was the trouble with women: even when they didn't have brains they seemed able to read a man's mind and, being so contrary by nature, they naturally couldn't stand it when a man no longer lusted after them.

By the time they had coffeed down the last of the pie the dining car was open to one and all, and it wouldn't have been fair to hog a table others were waiting for. So he had to take her back to the coach. Now that he'd had just about made up his mind to pass on this one, Penny seemed to require even more assistance in navigation and, no matter how polite he tried to grab her, she somehow managed to offer a handhold a man just wasn't supposed to put his hand on till he knew a lady a lot better. He couldn't help responding with a friendly tweak the last few times. So, of course, by the time they got back to their coach seats she was sure enough of herself again to demand the window seat with a pout he hardly felt the situation called for. He'd have given almost anyone the infernal seat had they just asked for it politely.

As he lapsed into weary silence again, the contrary little gal commenced to gush about how pretty the sunset was acting up outside. Longarm had seen the sun sink behind the Front Range more than once. He looked the other way and caught the old gal across the aisle shooting daggers at him before she locked eyes with him, wrinkled up her ugly face even worse, and looked away.

They were seated almost at conversing distance. Longarm was tempted to tell her she was dead wrong about his future plans for the evening. But he didn't. The poor prune-eyed bag of bones already seemed to hate men enough. He couldn't see why. She didn't look like a gal who'd been thrown down and ravaged by brutes all that much.

Pueblo wasn't half as far south of Denver as it felt like it was that evening. Longarm was sure they had somehow overshot Pueblo and were slowly approaching the Mexican border when at last the fool train pulled into the smoky smelter town. He was stuck with his offer to help Miss Penny Twinkles change trains, curse her sweet hide. So he took charge of her tickets and baggage checks, told her he'd meet her on the eastbound, and lit out, lest she shove a tit in his fool face climbing down the steps.

There wasn't all that much to changing trains, despite the confusion in the crowded depot. Longarm just scouted up a redcap he knew, handed him a quarter along with the paperwork, and went to the men's room to get rid of that extra coffee she had demanded. It was likely just as well he was coffeed up good. He would be getting off at Dodge around one or two A.M., depending on how

19

brave the engineer was, and it hurt worse to get up early than it did to just stay awake. He wondered if the dancing gal had put away all that coffee because she planned on being awake a lot that night.

Out on the crowded and confused platform he failed to spot Penny ready to board the eastbound. But the ugly old gal who hated him so much was standing there with a carpetbag, looking around wild-eyed, as if she was lost. Longarm went over, ticked the brim of his hat to her, and said, "If you're looking for the eastbound, ma'am, this is it."

She stared at him in silent amazement, but managed a stiff nod. He grabbed her bag away from her and said, "Let's get you aboard, then. Careful of them steps. I'd best give you a boost."

She must not have wanted him to grab her, even by the elbow, for she scooted up the steel steps like a mountain goat with its tail on fire. Longarm chuckled and followed more sedately with her luggage, knowing his and Penny's would be dealt with more sensibly by gents who did such chores for a living. As he followed the old gal into the Pullman corridor she suddenly turned with another nod that could have been meant as a grudging thank you and snatched her bag from him to vanish with it into the ladies' lounge.

He went on back to the more open center of the car where, sure enough, Penny had taken a window seat. He took out her tickets, read her seat number, and told her she had to move back a couple.

She acted like she expected him to help her get there, even though the train wasn't moving yet, so he did. He sat her down, handed over her tickets and claim checks, and said, "There you go. They'll be making up this

20

sleeping car for sleeping by nine, so I reckon this is *adios*."

She looked up at him as if he had just turned into a pumpkin and commanded him to sit down, for heaven's sake, and explain what on earth was going on. He took the seat facing hers and said, "It ain't all that complicated, Miss Penny. As you can see, there ain't many passengers in this car. So you won't have to worry about anyone who snores grabbing the top bunk above you when the porter makes up the bunks."

"Custis, I never bought a Pullman ticket. I was planning on just getting by as best I could in a coach seat, unless something turned up."

He nodded pleasantly. "Something did. I told you I had pull with the railroad, and you can see how few other passengers booked a Pullman bunk to K.C. You might want to slip a dime to the porter when he makes up this berth for you. Otherwise, it's on the house."

She didn't look grateful. She looked confused as hell as she asked him where he planned on spending the night. He told her, "I'm getting off at Dodge, like I said. It's hardly worth shucking one's boots to climb into a bunk between after-nine and before-three. So I booked myself coach a car or so back."

"Oh," she replied in a sad little voice. Then she dimpled at him coyly and added, "You don't have to go right *now*, do you? If this whole little nook is all mine, you can sit right there as my guest, can't you?"

He could, he knew. He was on good terms with the train crew and wouldn't have any trouble with them if he rode all the way to Dodge *behind* the green canvas hangings with Penny. But a man had to consider the trouble he might have with a difficult brunette in the wee small hours when it was time to dismount. He couldn't tell if she was a screamer, but he'd had gals scream on him who had started out behaving better, so there were times it just made more sense to get up from the table before the game got rough.

The train started up and the voluptuous little pest said something about not knowing what to tell the conductor if he wanted to ask tricky questions about her ticket. Longarm leaned back and reached for a smoke as he told her he would take care of the matter. He naturally asked her permission to light up, and she said she didn't mind. He had just got it going when the older, uglier gal came back and took a nearby seat, not looking at them. She was staring at her Pullman ticket as if she hoped it was some mistake, so Longarm forgave her for sitting so near them again. The poor old priss was probably even more disgusted. He chuckled, picturing the dirty pictures the old bat was making up about a younger gal and a gent whose heart was pure.

It might not have stayed so pure had not Penny caught a whiff of his cheroot smoke and wrinkled her pert nose so snooty. She was too polite or too uncertain of herself right now to tell him right out that she found his taste in tobacco uncouth, but he got her message. He snuffed the cheroot out on the heel of his old army boot and put it away, muttering, "I'd best finish this in the coach. This brand was meant to burn good in a stiff wind. I reckon it's a mite cow to smoke in refined surroundings."

She sighed. "Are you mad at me, Custis?" she asked.

He shook his head. "Resignation would describe my emotions closer to home, Miss Penny. I gave up getting mad at women long ago. I don't cuss the weather or worry as much about the hereafter as I used to, either. There's some things a grown man just has to face as facts he can't do nothing to change."

"You *are* mad. I can tell. Your eyes aren't looking at me any more. You're looking right through me, like I was a ghost!"

He didn't answer. He never lied when he had no good reason. The conductor saved the awkward situation by coming in just then to call out cheerfully about the time they were making that night. Longarm turned in his seat as if he had never watched a conductor punch tickets before, so Penny couldn't even pout at him for a spell. But all good things must come to an end, and the conductor made no trouble at all as he nodded to his old pal, Longarm, and told him with a wink that the bunks would be made up directly.

As soon as they were alone together again the dancer giggled and whispered, "I think he thinks we mean to be naughty in our own little lovey-dovey nest, don't you?"

He growled, "Don't whisper so, unless you want everyone else in this car to feel sure we are. I'd best make a grand and public exit before they start hanging up the drapes. Folks who ride Pullman regular suspicion all sorts of hanky-panky once the drapes are up and the lights are low. So I'd best not even be in this car when they trim the lamps."

He started to rise. She grabbed him by the thigh so hard her nails dug through the tweed like kitten claws and hissed, "Are you crazy? Can't you see I want you so bad I can taste it, you fool?"

He gently removed her hand from his thigh before blood poisoning could set in, kissed the back of it, and murmured back, "I know I must be a fool, for many a gal has told me I was, no matter which way I played the cards she dealt me. If it's any comfort, Miss Penny, I think you're pretty, and your offer is tempting as hell. But, like I said, I'm getting off at Dodge."

"For God's sake, this train won't get there until after midnight!"

"I know. Don't try to figure me out, honey. I gave up trying to figure gals like you out before I got to shaving regular."

She stared up, smiling fit to bust, but her eyes were cold. "Oh, I get it. You're one of those men who don't like *girls,* right?" she sneered.

He laughed like hell. Then, knowing they were attracting more attention than the truth of the matter called for, he just looked sheepish, asked her to keep it a secret, and got out of there as quick as he could.

It didn't take him long, riding back in the coach car, to wonder if he'd made such a good move, after all. The coach was crowded, some poor gal was traveling with a crying baby, and, worse yet, a fool with a harmonica was trying to play "Marching Through Georgia" and getting it wrong. Longarm considered going back there and informing the dumb young cowhand he'd ridden for the South, but that was likely get him to playing "Dixie" off-key, and it would sound dumb to say he'd ridden for the North as well.

The young mother with the crying baby would likely take it all wrong if he went back and told her he knew of an empty top bunk she and the kid could flop in. Besides, he wasn't really that sore at old Penny. She couldn't help being an annoying critter any more than that poor baby could. They were both just driven by the same dumb desire to have everything their own way. In fact, the more he thought about that poor lonesome brunette up forward, the less he found himself hating her. The hell of it was, a man couldn't even jerk off, riding

24

coach, and Dodge was still hours away.

But a man had to do what a man had to do and his orders were to travel east attracting as little attention as possible. So he sat tight as long as he could stand it, then went on back to the club car to steady his resolve. The club car was crowded and the beer was flat. It got worse a while later when the train crossed the Kansas line and the barkeep said they were all welcome to just sit there and smoke, but that the goddamned bar was closed. Longarm knew why, so he didn't join the howl or protest. When a morose gent standing next to him suggested lynching the barkeep, Longarm explained, "Wouldn't do no good. Kansas is a dry state."

"Hell, *everything's* dry out this way," the other man snorted. "But why can't I get another *drink?*"

"I ain't talking about parched prairie, pard," Longarm said. "The fuddy-duddy Kansas state government prohibits the consumption of anything stronger than lemonade this side of K.C., see?"

"Oh, Lord have mercy! Why on earth would anyone want to pass a fool law like that? How do folks get drunk in Kansas if they can't buy liquor?"

Longarm shrugged. "It ain't as serious as that. The law only applies to open state-held territory. Towns like Dodge and such have their own municipal ordinances on the subject. You can still get as drunk as you like in Dodge, as long as you don't shoot nobody."

He didn't feel like talking to greenhorns about other grim facts of life a man just had to grin and bear, so he went back up the train to his coach. He had to take another leak, so he moved on up to the gents' at the head of the car. It was taken. He shrugged and moved on to the one in the Pullman car ahead. He relieved himself and told his semi-erection to just hesh when it tried to remind him a likely naked gal was bunked alone, and likely wide awake, just a few yards closer to the engine.

But he was still in the rear corridor of Penny's car when all hell broke loose behind him. Longarm's double-action .44 was out and in his hand before the last of the roaring gunshots they'd been jarred by echoed away. Passengers of both sexes were screaming fit to bust as Longarm came up between the swaying green canvas curtains, shouting, "Everybody in your damn bunks! I'm the law! I'll deal with it!"

Someone yanked the emergency cord. Longarm almost landed flat on his face in the aisle, and would have, had not he grabbed at a drape with his free hand. As the train ground to a halt he saw that he'd ripped the curtain partly open. He told the naked lady in back of it he was sorry as hell and moved on into the cloud of blue gun-smoke lingering in the center of the car, right by Penny Twinkles' berth.

He said, "Come on, God, that just ain't fair!" as he tore open the bullet-riddled drapes. But the little brunette dancer lay there just the same, stark naked under a blood-soaked sheet, with her eyes staring up at him, looking confused as well as dead.

He reached in to haul the bloody sheet up over her bare tits and still pretty face, cursing softly. The conductor joined him to ask what was going on. That was fair, but everyone else was trying to talk as well at the same time.

Longarm held up a hand for silence. "Simmer down," he said. "The lady who was riding in this berth is dead. The next thing we need to know is whether anyone *else* is. You'd best call the roll, Conductor!"

The only Pullman passenger still unaccounted for was the mean-faced old woman in the bunk catty-corner from

Penny's. Longarm wasn't half as surprised as everyone else was when he yanked the drapes open to find nary a soul in her rumpled bunk. He holstered his own sidearm as he picked up a brass shell casing one would hardly expect to find on the pillow of an old maid and growled, "She was reloading as she rolled out of here, if it was a *she*. Whoever it was got to the far end of this car before anyone came in the other way, yanked the brake cord, and leaped off. If anyone with a horse was waiting, he or she is long gone. Even if the murderous whatever lit out on foot, tracking across spring grass is tough even by daylight, which it ain't outside."

The conductor said, "She must have been a lunatic. I got her name here somewheres, if you need it, Longarm."

"I do. It's likely a made-up name, but the law at the next stop will want all the details we can give 'em. We can talk about it along the way. We'd best get this train moving again. I sure hope they got a good undertaker in ... What's the next stop, Pete?"

"Cimarron. Wouldn't it make as much sense to carry the body as far as Dodge, Longarm? Cimarron ain't much, you know."

Longarm shook his head grimly. "It's the county seat," he said. "The killer killed her and leaped off in said county. So the sheriff of Gray County ought to know and ought to be doing something about it."

27

Chapter 3

The conductor had been right about Cimarron being little more than a prairie jerkwater stop. But the sheriff lived in town and, better yet, formed a posse at once to ride back along the rail line and scout for sign. The gent who acted as town mortician when he wasn't cutting hair opined he could fix the dead gal so she would keep well enough till her folks back East could send for her. They got her address and such from among the pathetic papers they found in her luggage. Penny Twinkles had kept a scrapbook showing all the places she had danced. There hadn't been all that many and her real name had been Jane Thurber. Her home address was a little town in Pennsylvania and the Western Union office in Cimarron said it was too small to have a telegraph office. So Long-arm paid the undertaker extra to embalm her good, even though it wasn't his federal duty and hence had to come out of his own pocket. When the undertaker asked if she'd been a friend of his he shook his head and answered, "Not hardly. But she might have been murdered because someone else thought we was closer than we really was. You pump her full of plenty of arsenic, hear? Pennsylvania's a long, lonesome trip in a baggage car, and there's no telling when they'll send for her."

The part-time undertaker said, "I'll use the new pink stuff we just got if it's all the same to you, Deputy. Arsenic makes 'em last forever but it turns 'em sort of dark."

Longarm shook his head and growled, "You do it like I say or we got no deal. It won't matter how dusky she gets in a dark box."

"You must get to open a lot of graves, Deputy."

"It goes with the job. That's how I know that sometimes the old ways is best, and a gal with a shape like she had deserves to keep it. Like I said, plenty of arsenic salts and a lead-lined box."

Having settled that and sent a wire to Denver informing the home office, Longarm had nothing much better to do in Cimarron. He left word for the sheriff to catch up with him by wire if the posse found anything. Then he caught a short ride aboard a late-night or, rather, early-morn freight. He jumped off in Dodge, just a few miles down the line, and sure enough, his Winchester and his other gear were waiting at the depot there.

He lugged them to the Alhambra Hotel near the better-known and noisier Alhambra Saloon. He found the night clerk asleep behind the desk. He yelled, "Wake up! It's morning, almost, and I'm looking for a jasper called T. S. Winslow. What does the T. S. stand for?"

The clerk rubbed his sleep-gummed eyes and muttered, "Tough shit, I reckon. I don't know the cuss, personal. Let's see what the book says."

He opened the hotel register, ran a dirty fingernail down the names, and said, "Here you go. T. S. Winslow—Room 216. But you can't go up without a bellhop, and the bellhop ain't here at this ungodsome hour. You want a room of your own, meantime?"

Longarm started to nod, thought better of it, and said, "I'd like to get out of Dodge as soon as I can, no offense. So I'll bet you two bits that you won't remember where old T. S. will be able to find me when and if he ever gets up."

The clerk picked up the quarter between them and put it away, saying, "You lose. Where do you mean to wait for this pilgrim, pard?"

"Is the Longbranch still open all night?"

"Sure. It never closes. Saves buying door locks, I reckon. I'll tell Winslow you'll be waiting for him in the Longbranch Saloon. How the two of you work it out from there on ain't no concern of mine. That *is* a double-action .44 I can't help noticing in that serious cross-draw rig under your frock coat, ain't it?"

Longarm chuckled and said, "It is, but don't worry about your paid-up guests. I'm law. Old T. S. and me are meeting friendly."

"Oh? Is he law, too?"

Longarm said that was close enough and headed back out to the street without further comment. A bird watcher wandering about Dodge had enough to worry about without the whole town knowing it.

It was just getting light and Longarm was just having second thoughts about the night's sleep he'd surrendered without a fight by the time he got to the Longbranch. As he had expected, it was open, but more depressing than he'd remembered, at that hour. There was only one other customer, sitting drunk or mighty tuckered at a table in the back. The Longbranch ran back about forty feet, but was no wider than a tobacco shop. With the lights so low it looked more like a railroad tunnel than a hellfire drinking establishment. The old gray barkeep perked up as he recognized Longarm of old and put his baseball bat back under the bar. Longarm said, "Morning, Sam. Could I leave this stuff behind the mahogany for now?"

Old Sam Grogan said, "Sure, Longarm. What else'll you have?"

"Would you haul that bat out again if I asked for *coffee*, Sam? I've had a long, hard night and the dawning day ain't shaping up as Sunday, neither. I got to stay awake at least until I can get me and some dude who's meeting me here aboard a train."

Grogan nodded and reached under the bar again. "Don't spread this about, but I never touch the stuff they serve as *booze* in this joint!"

So the two of them were sharing cold black coffee when, about half an hour later, a kid came in from outside to ask which one of them might be Deputy U. S. Marshal Long. Longarm pleaded guilty and the kid said, "A lady sent me in to fetch you, Deputy. She says she can't come in such a disreputatious place and wants you to come *out,* pronto!"

Longarm frowned thoughtfully down at the young messenger and replied, "Do tell? Would this mysterious as well as snooty lady happen to be tall, skinny, and sort of old and ugly? I got a reason for asking, son."

The boy shook his head. "This one's a real looker. I don't know how old she is, but she sure ain't tall or ugly."

Longarm still didn't like it. He hadn't told many people he would be in Dodge that morning, let alone just where, and they had tried to set him up once, so far, with a mighty tough woman or a man dressed mighty sissy.

31

He told the kid to stay inside with Sam as he moved to the batwing doors for a cautious gaze at the sunrise.

There was nobody in sight but a sure enough she-male, standing prissy backed by a watering trough out front, as if that was as close as she dared to approach such a place as the Longbranch. She wasn't pointing a gun at anyone, so Longarm left his own where it was as he strode out to join her. As he got a better look he saw that she was even better-looking than the late Penny Twinkles, albeit built more skinny and more severely dressed in a whipcord travel duster and veiled black hat. He asked her who she was and who might have told her where he was. She snapped, "The room clerk at my hotel told me you said to meet you here. Couldn't you have picked a more refined meeting place, Marshal Long?"

He said, "I'm only a deputy marshal, and you can't be..."

"I'm T. S. Winslow of the Smithsonian Institute," she said. "Who were you expecting to meet here?"

He laughed and said, "I wouldn't ask any lady to meet me in the Longbranch, Miss Winslow. You see, I thought you was a *he* bird watcher, not a *she* bird watcher!"

"I'm neither. I'm an ornithologist for the Smithsonian Institute. You do know what the Smithsonian Institute is, don't you?"

"I even know what an ornithologist is, Miss Winslow. I can read. Like I said, you're a bird watcher, no matter how fancy you spell it."

"And you, sir, are a drunken lout! I don't understand why they said I was to come with you to that disgusting business along the Arkansas. I'm perfectly capable of finding my own way."

He nodded. "I'm sure you are, ma'am. I don't know why they saddled us with one another, neither, but I ain't drunk, I'm just tired as hell. Are you ready to move on now, or do you just want to cuss me some more?"

She favored him with a slight smile and replied, "If we have to travel together we may as well get it over with. I'm all packed at my hotel. You?"

He told her to sit tight and ran inside to get his own gear. She had done no such thing, he saw, as he rejoined her. She was standing ramrod stiff and muttering as he fell in beside her to offer her his free arm. He was just being polite, of course.

To his mild surprise, she took it. He had to grant her a good mark for knowing how a real lady was supposed to act, whether she fancied the company of her escort or not. They went back to her hotel. She insisted on hiring a buckboard for their combined gear and offered to pay when he said it didn't look like all that much. He had, in fact, expected even a he bird watcher to travel loaded down with all sorts of scientific junk. But old T. S. must have really been used to traveling, for she kept things down to a couple of satchels and an old army foot locker.

When he insisted he could balance the fair-sized foot locker on his free shoulder she told him he was a fool but, in the end, followed after him toting her own heavy satchels. So probably her initials didn't stand for Tough Shit after all.

While they waited for the next eastbound, he explained the route to Tangleroost, since it was sort of hard to get to from anywhere sensible. Then, once he saw that she was looking a mite worried, he suggested, "Maybe it would be best if you sort of holed up in K.C. and let me go the rest of the way on the careful lonesome, Miss Winslow. I wouldn't want to ship another lady back East in a box, and I've good reason to suspicion someone's gunning for me."

33

She frowned up at him and replied, "Oh, you too? I thought they'd sent you to guard me because they thought *I* was in some danger."

He frowned right back at her. "What kind of danger are you supposed to be in, Miss Winslow? I sure wish my office would let me in on such matters *ahead* of time!"

She shrugged. "I think the Institute's just overexcited. I had to send them a report, of course, when some of my field notes were stolen, and then there was the time some moron took a shot at me out on the prairie..."

"Somebody's been gunning for *you,* too?"

"I don't think it's as serious as all that. It was probably just a kid hunting jackrabbits. There was only one shot, fired well over me as I was riding in a low draw. By the time I loped my pony up to the top of the rise there was nobody in sight. I don't think it was meant as a serious attack."

He shook his head and insisted, "Any attack involving a bullet near a human skull sounds serious, Miss Winslow. Were you out there unarmed as well as solo?"

She shrugged. "Well, of course I had my saddle gun out by the time I got to the top of the rise. But surely a girl alone..."

He shrugged and said, "It depends on how tough you look with a gun, I reckon. Somehow I just can't picture it right now. Do you mind if I sort of sit on your foot locker a spell, Miss Winslow? I don't know what's wrong with me this morning. I've gone seventy-two hours without sleep and it *still* felt better."

She nodded and he sat down. It didn't help as much as he had hoped it would. He reached absently for a smoke as she hunkered down beside him, put a cool hand to his brow, and asked, "Are you ill? You don't seem to

34

be running a fever, but I don't like your coloring at all!"

He stared owlishly at her and replied defensively, "You sure are one to talk, little darling. I like red hair and you can't help having red eyes, but that fire-engine-red duster ain't my notion of modest attire."

She frowned. "My hair and eyes are light brown," she told him, "and my duster's tan. You're turning a ghastly shade of mustard under that deep suntan! We have to get you to a doctor! You're either sick or worse!"

He shook his head and lit his cheroot with the railroad flare he had somehow found among the waterproof matches he usually packed in his frock coat. But the cheroot tasted just awful, and he said, "It serves me right for lighting up in front of a lady without her permission. How come I forgot to, and what's worse than being sick?"

She put her hand to his face and raised an eyelid before she replied, "I think you may have been poisoned. Your eyes are so dilated it's a wonder you can still see at all. Put your head down between your knees, and I'll run for a doctor, Mr. Long!"

"Aw, call me Custis, you sweet little thing. I don't want no doctor. I hear the train a-coming, and we got to git on board. I forget why, but Billy Vail said it was important."

She had naturally heard the approaching train, too, but she insisted, "You're too ill to stand, let alone board a train. And will you please get rid of that foul cigar before you puke?"

He tossed the cheroot aside, muttering, "There you go. Now stand back and let me up. For we got to catch that train."

"Damn it, Custis..."

"Damn me no damns, little darling. I know I've been poisoned, if this ain't the Black Plague. But we're going to Tangleroost anyway. That'll learn the sissy who's been trying to stop us from getting there."

As he rose he knew he was about to puke, fall down, or just die. But he didn't want to do any of them, so he didn't, although the next few million years felt confusing as hell.

As he was flying across the border with the rest of the wild geese, Longarm looked down and saw that, sure enough, they'd painted all the grass in Canada pink and all the grass in the U. S. yellow, just like it was on most maps. But there was still something wrong here. He turned to the snow goose flying next to him and honked, "Pardon me, ma'am, but how come we're all flying *south* this spring? Shouldn't we be headed the other way?"

The snow goose with the big brown eyes replied, "Who ever heard of wild geese flying any way but south? Don't you have any poetry in your soul? It's the red, red *robins* that fly *north* in the spring, you fool!"

That sounded fair. He was glad he wasn't a robin. He knew he would just starve before he ever ate one single worm, as sick as he felt to his stomach right now. He asked the pretty snow goose, "Why don't we land on that big blue lake they've painted down there, little darling?"

She sniffed and said, "Don't get fresh. It's not the breeding season yet."

He shook his head wearily and told her, "I wish you gals would wait till a man got fresh before you told him not to get fresh. No offense, but that wasn't what I had in mind at all. I ain't sure how I'd manage with a bird in the first damn place, and in the second damn place, I'm a lawman sworn to uphold the law, and bestiality can get you twenty years!"

Naturally, being a contrary she-male, even if she was a bird, the snow goose sniffed and pouted, "Who are you calling a beast, you brute? I guess I'm as fine a piece of feathered ass as you'll find in this infernal flock! So there!"

He didn't want to argue. He just needed a lake full of fresh water, fast, to wash the awful taste out of his mouth. So he dropped down to get some. But the snow goose followed, honking, "You can't drink that, you fool. Can't you see it's just blue ink on paper? You sure are acting odd for a *bird* this morning!"

He frowned thoughtfully and said, "I ain't no bird. I'm Deputy U. S. Marshal Custis Long, Miss Snow Goose."

"Oh, yeah? Then what are you doing up here in the sky with us?"

It was a good question. He had no sensible answer, so he opened his eyes to find out where he really might be.

He was aboard a train, stretched out on a bunk, and naked from the waist up. He wondered how come, so he raised his head from the pillow to look around. It felt as if his skull was made of solid lead, but he saw now that he was in a private compartment with good old T. S. The bird-watching gal had taken off her duster and was seated by the window in a blue polka-dot dress with white buttons up one side of the skirt. She had removed her hat and veil and, sure enough, her unbound hair was the color of the cornsilk he used to smoke behind the barn when he was a kid. The notion of smoking made him retch, and she glanced his way. She gasped, "Oh, you're awake at last! How do you feel?"

"Awful," he said. "How did I get up here on this top bunk, and what happened to my shirt and so forth, Miss Winslow?"

"The porters helped," she said. "I asked the conductor to see if there was a doctor on the train. There wasn't, so I had to do the best I could. Your frock coat, hat, and guns are hanging in the closet. One of the porters said he'd try to clean your vest and shirt up forward. Don't worry, I took the watch and derringer from your vest before I gave it to him."

"What did I do, puke all over myself?"

"My duster's being cleaned, too. I fear I may have overdone the universal antidote I forced down you, but I see that it seems to have worked."

He propped himself up on one elbow and asked her what she was talking about, adding, "Are you an M.D. as well as a T. S.?"

She dimpled and said, "My first name's Tess. I'm not a doctor, but I do have a degree in biology. I mixed milk with baking soda, mustard, and ground charcoal, to absorb the poison, get it up, or both. From the smell of what came out of you, I'd say someone dosed you with some powerful vegetable alkaloid. You must be strong as a bull. I was sure you'd be unconscious all the way to Kansas City, and we're not halfway there yet."

He grimaced and replied, "As a matter of fact, I feel weak as a kitten. But let's study on this poison notion, Tess. I don't see how anyone could have poisoned me, recent."

She shrugged and said, "Don't look at me. You were looking green around the gills the first moment I saw you. Frankly, I thought you were drunk."

He shook his head. "I told you I wasn't, damn it. Let's see, now. It couldn't have been Miss Chipmunk

Alice, for I refused the drink she offered, and that was twenty-four hours ago, in any case. How long does such stuff take to act, by the way?"

"I've no idea. I don't even know which of several related alkaloids you may have been poisoned with. It could have been foxglove, henbane, or even morning glory, from the symptoms. I don't think any of them would take more than a few hours to hit you, though. Were you drinking much alcohol last night?"

He smiled wanly and said, "Matter of fact, I was drinking less than usual. Knowing I'd be up a spell, I stuck mostly to black coffee. Why?"

She said, "That's probably why you're still alive, then. Caffeine is at least a mild antidote to most alkaloid depressants. Hard liquor on top of say, wolfsbane will kill you for sure."

"Hmm . . . some rascal who had me down as a harder drinker than I was might have planned on that, not wanting to be about to answer questions when I went down. Let's see, now. I ate supper sitting across a table from Penny Twinkles, so I'd have likely noticed if she'd been powdering my grub. I had a beer or more in the club car later, but nobody even flicked cigar ash in the schooner I was holding, and the State of Kansas kept me from drinking all that many, bless its blue nose. I didn't eat or drink nothing in Cimarron. I had a mess of black coffee, waiting for you in the Longbranch. Can't see old Sam Grogan as a member of the Borgia family and, no offense, poisoning is usually a she-male crime, in any case."

She wrinkled her nose and replied, "I must say you do meet odd members of my sex. Chipmunk Alice and Twinkles?"

He grinned sheepishly and said, "I don't think *either*

39

of 'em poisoned me. So who's left?"

"What about the people who served you aboard that other train?"

He considered, shook his head, and said, "I get along tolerably with colored folk. I've ridden with that same crew too often to suspicion them of deciding to murder me at this late date. The thing that works best is a mighty *slow* poison. . . . But, damn it, that changes the picture entirely!"

She stared up at him, puzzled, so he explained, "I ate a good breakfast yesterday at a stand-up chili counter. Helped myself to the free lunch at the Parthenon near the federal building around noon. Both meals were eaten under elbow-bumping conditions. So I just can't say whether anyone was salting my grub along with his or not."

She nodded. "Some poisons take as long as three full days to take effect, speaking of the Borgias. But why do you say it changes the picture, Custis? Attempted murder is attempted murder, no?"

He started to sit up all the way, gave it up as a disgusting notion, and told her, "I wasn't told about this bird watching nonsense until *after* I'd eaten my last suspicious meal. So it was likely just a coward's way of getting me for some other reason. I've been packing a badge six or eight years now, and you'd be surprised how many folk take it personally when I'm just doing my job. Most of 'em are just funning, of course, when they swear in court they'll get me as soon as they get out, but from time to time I meet one who's a caution when it comes to holding a grudge."

He tried to get some spit going in his dry mouth, gave it up as a futile attempt, and said, "There you go. Mayhaps the bullet that made you so thoughtful was just a rabbit hunter, after all. Do we have any drinking water in here?"

She rose, went to the corner sink, and poured him a tin cup of tepid water. As she handed it to him, she asked, "What about those notes of mine that were stolen?"

He didn't answer until he'd swallowed the whole cup. Who would have thought Pullman water could taste so fine? He handed back the cup and asked if he could have another. "Don't know. Tell me about the papers as got stolen."

She handed back the refilled cup as she explained, "They took three whole notebooks filled with field observations. I don't see what anyone but an ornithologist would want with them. My specialty is extinction, or, rather, why some species become extinct while others don't."

He was sorry he had asked, but since he had, he swallowed the last of the water and said, "That ain't no mystery, no offense. I was there when the last of the buffalo was shot south of the U.P. line. There ain't much of the *north* herd left, either. Shoot enough critters, and they just naturally ain't *there* no more, right?"

"Wrong," she said. "It's not that simple. What about wolves and coyotes?"

"What *about* 'em? They're both considered pests by most."

"That's true, and every state I know of pays a bounty on both species at the moment. They're both wild canines. They're both shot on sight. The wolf is getting rarer every year, but the coyote is increasing its range as well as its numbers. Nobody can tell me why, and please don't say it's because the coyote is smarter or a smaller target. It has to be more complicated than that."

"I thought your field was birds, Tess."

"It is. The Smithsonian wants me to apply my research to the migrating birds of the central flyway, which is why we're on our way to Tangleroost right now. But there has to be some common law of nature involved. Nobody knows why some species seem to become extinct while others thrive under persecution. That idiotic shooting contest in the hitherto natural roosting place for hundreds of species may give us a few clues."

Just thinking about a swamp full of dead ducks put Longarm's head back on the pillow, but Tess had warmed up to the subject and continued. "We tried to *stop* the insane shootoff, of course. But as long as they're bound and determined, the Institute thinks it may give us a controlled experiment we'd never dream of doing ourselves. They say over a thousand would-be Nimrods have signed up to slaughter migrating birds, all in that one small area."

He gagged and groaned, "All right, I'll look at the gunslicks and you look at the birds. It sounds disgusting either way."

"I'm sure it will be," she said. "The question is which species will survive the unusual stress."

"Well, if I spot any hunters who are wanted for more serious crimes, I can tell you what's likely to happen to *them*, at least. I promise not to shoot no kee-kee birds, Tess."

She smiled thoughtfully at him and said, "I must say your attitude is a refreshing change, Custis. Most men of your background just can't seem to resist letting fly at any moving target, for some reason."

He grimaced and replied, "There ain't nothing odd

about my background. I was born to decent enough parents, I reckon. As to why some old country boys feel proud to shoot sparrows, it's likely they never got to fight in a war. There's nothing like a war to make a growing boy *pay attention* to what he's shooting at. I wouldn't want you to think I was a nature lover, Tess. I've shot my share of eating critters and pests, four-legged or two. But I learned long ago not to waste ammo on critters that are no use to me dead."

She nodded and said, "That's still a refreshing change from most red blooded he-men. I'm not a sissy, either. I shoot game for the pot or as specimens. I simply feel it's a terrible waste to kill anything needlessly. And some species are actually on their way to total extinction, at the rate we're going. I've been doing studies on the passenger pigeon, for instance, and—"

"Hold on," he cut in with a dry laugh, remembering an awful harvest time in his West-By-God-Virginia boyhood. "If there's one infernal bird you don't have to worry your pretty little head about it's the *passenger*, Tess! One fall a flock of 'em landed in my daddy's orchard and I was there. So don't tell me I'm a fibber when I tell you them pesky pigeons wrecked our fruit crop entire! We did all we could to stop 'em, but they just kept coming and coming until their weight busted tree limbs down on us and we had to retreat for our lives. I don't know how many of them chose our orchard to flatten that fall. But we carted away wagons full of dead ones we'd killed trying to save our trees. I'm sure at least a hundred times as many flew away, once they saw we meant business!"

She nodded soberly and said, "Early accounts tell of flocks ten miles wide flying over from south horizon to north, close-packed."

"There you go. There has to be *millions* of passengers

in every flock, and the Lord knows how many *flocks* there are. So how come you think they're *extinct,* for Pete's sake?"

"There are still millions, maybe billions, but they're no longer seen in many parts of the country, so their numbers must be dropping alarmingly."

"Well, the ones I've seen up to now surely have been alarming. But it stands to reason the market hunters have reduced 'em to more reasonable numbers."

She shook her head. "It's more complicated than that. We know how many passengers have been smoked or pickled. We know that for every game bird shot, at least a dozen more have been blown out of the sky by casual marksmen just for the heck of it. But the numbers don't add up, Custis. In recent years market hunting has fallen off, but some species of game birds still seem to be dwindling away while, at the same time, others are increasing. There are twice as many crows in the midwest today than early settlers reported. The ivory-bill woodpecker is getting so rare some naturalists have never seen one, and we both know nobody shoots woodpeckers for the pot. The Carolina parakeet is gone for good. Don't say they were shot off. The same Southern farmers have been trying to wipe out the rice bird harder, and so far they can't seem to make a dent in its numbers. The whooping crane is getting rare, yet the sand hill crane, as good a target, seems to thrive on being shot at by every farm boy with a .22. I don't think hunting pressure is the answer. But, as I said, the big shootoff in the Tangleroost may give us some leads. Some migrating birds must be doing something right. If we could only find out what that was, we might be able to save the *others* before it's too late!"

44

Longarm didn't answer. Now that he felt better, he just wanted to sleep a month of Sundays. But he sure had some funny dreams on the way to Kansas City.

Chapter 4

When Tess had to wake him up, rolling through the K.C. Yards, Longarm felt good as new. Or at least he did until he was up and dressed. He allowed he might let the redcaps handle all their luggage just this once.

His legs felt sort of rubbery as they transferred to the dinky line they would have to take south to Fort Smith. Their southbound wasn't due to leave for over an hour, so they had plenty of time to grab a bite in the depot dining hall. Tess warned him against a steak smothered in hot chili after all he'd been through, but he said he was hungry as a wolf and that chili had never killed him yet. He didn't ask why she'd draped her travel duster over the back of her chair. His own shirt was still damp. But it made up for the stuffy steam heat in the crowded joint.

By the time he was enjoying his after-pie coffee and a smoke, he was feeling almost human again. He took out his watch and said, "Well, we've still got plenty of time to kill. Would you like another slice of pie?"

She laughed and asked where she'd ever put it. Then she excused herself from the table to wash her hands.

He gazed after her fondly as she left the table. He admired polka dots, no matter which side of a gal they were on. He noticed an ugly rascal at another table staring at her retreating rear view, too. There wasn't anything Longarm could do about it, since admiring a handsome figure wasn't a federal offense, but he stared harder at the other man anyway. He was sure he'd seen that ugly face somewhere before, recently, but try as he might, he couldn't match it up with any Wanted fliers. He knew he'd have never forgotten an outlaw that ugly.

Longarm finished his coffee and took another drag on his cheroot. He wished Tess would get cracking with those hands she had to wash, for it was stuffy as hell in here and he needed fresh air, bad. The heavy meal had made him drowsy. Or had it? He hadn't eaten all that much, and he'd been sleeping for hours on that other train. He loosened his collar and snuffed his smoke out, shaking his head to clear it. At the other table the other man was rising slowly with his gun out. The son of a bitch had drawn it under cover of his own tablecloth.

Longarm slid sideways off his chair and went for his own sidearm as, all around, folk started screaming scared and tinny, like they all had buckets over their heads. Longarm could read the killing intentions of that towering bastard, too, but for some fool reason his own gun hand barely seemed to be moving through the glue-thick air. The other's gun muzzle rose, slow as a lazy hog's snout from the trough, and grew a big red rose of flame out its end, in the same impossible slow motion.

By this time Longarm was sprawled sideways on the tile floor. He figured that first shot must have missed him when he heard a long, low rumble of breaking glass somewhere behind him. He had his own hand on his gun grips now, but some son of a bitch would seem to have

47

poured melted tar in his damned holster, judging from the way his .44 was coming out, too slow to save him, as that red-eyed rascal's gun muzzle trained on him again.

Then in the same dreamy, slow way, the side of the gunslick's head evaporated in a big frothy cloud of strawberry jam. Then he dropped out from under his own dark Stetson to beat it and his shattered brains to the floor, no matter how long it seemed to take him to get there. A deep, hollow voice boomed, "Custis, are you hurt?"

He looked up at Tess to answer weakly, "Nope, but I reckon I'm poisoned again. Where did you get that gun, Tess?"

She lowered her smoking S&W to her side as she knelt over him. He could see by the shapely thigh exposed by the slit of her unbuttoned skirt how she'd got to her garter holster so good. She said, in a slightly more normal voice, "That man was trying to kill you!"

He said, "I noticed. It's a good thing you don't spend as much time in the ladies' room as he expected. For he done it *again,* the sneaky bastard. I wish I knowed *how!*"

As Tess tried to help Longarm up, she was joined by a K.C. copper badge, who did it better but demanded to know why a dead man was lying on the floor just a few feet away. Longarm said, "I'm law, and she's with me. Let me look at *him* some more and I may be able to tell you better."

The other customers had cleared out, some without paying, by the time Tess and the K.C. copper had Longarm standing over the man she had just shot. Longarm stared down, nodded, and said, "Last night this gent was dressed up like a woman. He tried to gun me while I was drugged or otherwise occupied. When that didn't work, he tried again, just now, and damn near made it.

48

He knew I'd been slipped more of whatever. I see now that he was biding his time and made his move just as I was fixing to fall down anyway. He must have wanted additional glory, the yellow-livered skunk."

Longarm shook his head to clear it and added, "What I still can't figure out is how he drugged me at long distance. Anyone can see he was seated too far off to sprinkle poison in my coffee. And it couldn't have been Miss Winslow, here. I was watching."

"Custis, what an awful thing to say! We'd better question the kitchen help!" Tess exclaimed.

The K.C. copper thought that was a grand notion, but Longarm shook his head. "Not hardly. How could the sneak have expected us to come here to eat? We didn't know *ourselves*, until we saw we had some time to kill. I sure wish you hadn't killed him so good, Tess. I'd give most anything to know the answer. For it makes me nervous as hell to be poisoned regular at long distance!"

By this time other local law had crowded in. Longarm was sure they would miss that other train, now. Big-city coppers could be so damned pesky about a private shootout. But then one of the newcomers said, "Hey, I know who that gent on the floor is! We just got a flier on him. He answered to Snake Simmons. I think his real name was Cedric. He was supposed to be doing twenty at hard for armed robbery, but the other day, when they looked in his cell, he was gone. The Pinkertons have already put a bounty out on him. They wanted him for other stuff they couldn't prove."

"Like hired gun?" asked Longarm.

The copper said, "Right. How did you know?"

"Just a lucky guess. But look here, gents, us federal men ain't allowed to claim rewards, cuss the unfairness of it all. So, if you all want to take care of the tedious paperwork, he's all yours. This lady and me have a train to catch."

The K.C. coppers had to talk it over some, but it didn't take them long. Less than an hour later, Longarm and Tess Winslow were aboard their southbound train. By now it was getting late, and it would get even later before they reached Fort Smith, but Longarm didn't see fit to mention booking another private compartment just yet. A man traveling with a woman he'd never even kissed had to play things by ear. There was plenty of time for her to say she was getting sleepy. Meanwhile he could just admire her, seated in the coach and enjoy a smoke or two.

As he took out a fresh cheroot and started to light it, Tess grabbed it right from his mouth and cried, "Don't you dare! That could be it!"

He stared at her, bemused, as she sniffed his stolen smoke, licked it, and sniffed it some more. She nodded grimly and said, "I thought so. It's henbane. You *must* be strong as a bull!"

He took the wet cheroot back and ran his moustache over it, sniffing deeply. He wasn't sure what henbane was supposed to smell like, but he'd been smoking the same brand for a long time, and it had never smelled so odd before. He put it away as evidence, saying, "I've been meaning to cut down on my smoking, anyway. But how in thunder do you poison a smoke in a man's own pocket?"

Tess asked where he had gotten them in the first place. He told her the Union Depot in Denver, and added that they had never sold him unusual three-for-a-nickel's before.

She arched an eyebrow at him and said, "Tell me about

this Chipmunk Alice and . . . 'ah . . . Twinkles you seem to know so well."

He grinned sheepishly. "I never got to know neither of them well enough for them to have picked my pockets, Tess. Old Alice was a police informant I wouldn't get that close to on a bet, and, while the late Penny Twinkles was more socially acceptable, I never got to kiss her before that rascal you just shot back there shot *her,* likely because he had a dirty mind."

"What if she was murdered to shut her up? What if she was his confederate?"

"Now you're just talking silly, Tess. Poor little Penny was too dumb to be a crook. Hell, she couldn't even pick up a desperate man on a train."

"Are you certain she never even brushed against you?"

"All sorts of folk brush against one getting on and off a train. But, hold it, I *did* help that gent you shot aboard the eastbound last night, thinking he was a she, that is. I don't recall either one of them picking my pocket. But, on the other hand, you ain't *supposed* to, are you?"

Tess nodded grimly and said, "Nobody had to pick your pocket. It's a lot easier to slip something *in* a pocket than to get it *out!"*

He frowned thoughtfully, reached under his vest, and took out the whole pack. Her notion was a good one. But it didn't work. Every cheroot he had on him smelled of henbane.

He sighed. "Damn, to think I paid extra to embalm that sassy little thing, too," he said.

Tess looked triumphant, for some reason. "Then you *did* have an affair with your pretty fellow passenger, after all!" she said.

He frowned. "No, I never. But, now that I think back on it, I was smoking about the last of my *old* cheroots

51

when we first met up. So she knew what pocket I carried fresh tobacco in. Going and coming from the dining car she did bump against me more than any other passenger could have got away with. So, as many a poor man can tell you, a gal don't have to even kiss him to get him in a whole lot of trouble. I wonder what they told her she was slipping in my poor innocent pocket? I know she needed money, but I still can't see her as a real criminal."

"Tell me just how she was murdered."

"Oh, that part's no mystery. The gunslick pretending to be an ugly old gal wasn't after her in particular. He thought we were sharing a Pullman berth together and just shot hell out of everyone who might have been in there. It's okay about the extra embalming. She was just a dupe they used to get at me."

Tess looked out the window at the lengthening shadows for a spell. Then she said, "I wouldn't want that to happen again. And we don't know how many could be in one the plot. Don't you think we'd be safer if we traveled private compartment?"

He nodded soberly. "I'll see what I can do with the conductor," he said.

Then she had to go and spoil it all by adding, *"Separate* compartments, of course. This time I really have to get some sleep."

He grinned sheepishly. "Of course. What sort of a rascal do you think I am, Miss Tess?"

She grinned right back. "I don't know. I have no idea what your Miss Twinkles looked like. But I know what *I* look like in my nightgown. So why tempt fate?"

He didn't fare any better aboard the riverboat they changed to at Fort Smith. He got some fresh tobacco, which she smelled and said was safe. But the infernal riverboat had more separate staterooms than one could shake a stick at. When she wasn't chawing his ear about endangered old birds or talking in circles about who had tried to stop them from counting them, she kept going to bed alone. Some gals were like that, and there was nothing much a man could do about it without making false promises. He knew she sort of liked him. She'd proven it by saving his life. But every time he brought up the breeding habits of more interesting species, she got to fretting about her damned old birds again. She said some folk back East were trying to get a law passed that prohibited the shooting of game birds during the breeding season, when they were most vulnerable to pressure, as she called shooting them. He said he had always known how hard it was for a robin to build a nest with birdshot in its red breast, and that it sure beat all how even humans got to feeling romantic in the spring. But, for a gal so interested in the billing and cooing of birds, she wouldn't bill and coo worth a damn.

He didn't get mad, but it sure made for a boring trip down the lower Arkansas. They had to catch another short-line train from the river landing to the town itself. As they rode through the dismal country between the river and the dinky jerkwater town in the middle of nowhere, it was hard to see what on earth a town was doing there.

Save for the railroad causeway, the deadwood swamp all around was too thin to plow and too thick to fish in. Tess said it had all been lowland hardwood forest until the natural levee had busted in some flood and drowned it all. The dead trees rose like mossy, leafless ghosts from black muck and scummy green puddles as far as the eye could see. Tess said the mud was still too acid for the usual cattails and water lilies to repair the damage this soon. She got all excited and clapped her hands when they passed a quarter acre of spring-green skunk cabbage. She said that was a good sign. He didn't argue. He'd learned as a kid that walking through skunk-cabbage patches was a good way to wind up with mighty stinky mud above your boot tops. She said all the dead trees were good for ivory bills and bluebirds, too. He didn't see either. For a bird sanctuary, the Big Tangleroost was mighty silent and spooky. When he commented on this she said to just wait, as the spring migration hadn't quite got off the ground yet. She said her fool birds were still down South somewhere, but that they would be along most any minute. He said he could hardly wait. He meant it disgusted, but she didn't get it. She said she was happy they had arrived ahead of time, too.

They passed an open stretch of oxbow lake scummed emerald green with floating duckweed. Then the combo stopped and the conductor came back to tell them they had as long as the engine up front drank water to get off. The baggage smashers had already tossed their gear out, up the splintery platform. Tess looked about, bewildered, and asked him, "Are you sure this is the right place? I was told there'd be a *town* here!"

It was a good question. The most imposing structure in sight was the water tower that gave the trains an excuse to stop there. They needed one. Save for a business block of whitewashed wood near the railroad tracks, the rest of Tangleroost town consisted of frame housing that would have caused a scandal on an Indian reserve.

The rutted, cinder-paved streets were overcrowded for a settlement so small, albeit not as crowded as Longarm had been led to expect with the big shootoff due to start in less than twenty-four hours. Most of the crowd acted as if it had seen a railroad train before, but a mess of gents in the bird-watching business ran a buckboard up to the platform as Tess yoo-hooed at them. She told Longarm they were her pals from the Smithsonian. He said it figured. Most of them were dressed sensibly enough, but one wore a deer-stalker's hat and another had mosquito netting hanging all around the brim of his white pith helmet. He reminded Longarm of a beekeeper—a scared one—but he seemed to be in charge. Tess introduced him as Bruce, and old Pith Helmet called Longarm "my good man" when he thanked him for getting Tess safely there. Longarm got the distinct impression he was being told his services were no longer needed. So, as her pals loaded Tess Winslow's gear onto the buckboard, Longarm picked up his own and headed for the hotel sign across the street.

When he asked the pimple-faced simp behind the pine desk what their rates might be, the clerk giggled like a gal and said, "Surely you jest, and we expect the real crowd to arrive tomorrow, when the shootoff starts official!"

Longarm rested his possibles and carbine on the desk as he asked the clerk if this particular hotel was it. The clerk said, "I'm afraid so. The honky-tonk next door rents beds by the hour, complete with hot and cold running whores. But I doubt you could afford a whole night at a time there. You used to be able to get laid around here for two bits. Now it'll cost you five bucks."

Longarm smiled crookedly. "Well, Lord knows they've waited for such a short-lived opportunity, poor critters. Before I go, could you tell me where everyone's went? I'll take your word on how crowded this town is today. But it didn't look *that* crowded *outside,* just now."

The clerk shrugged and said he guessed most of the contestants were out in the swamp, hunting. Longarm frowned. "I thought we'd agreed the big shootoff don't start until tomorrow," he said.

The clerk giggled again and confided, "You know that and I know that, but do the contest judges know that? They ain't arrived yet. Each day's prize will be for the total bag in each gunner's game sack. Can you tell a day-old dead duck from one as just gave up the ghost?"

Longarm nodded, picked up his gear, and went out to find the nearest Western Union office. If he wired his home office he was here, they might wire Marshal Moran the same. It hardly made sense for a man working under cover to wander all about asking where in thunder the rest of the law might be hereabouts. But he'd just spied the hanging sign at the far end of the business block when an all-too-familiar female voice called out, "Longarm, you sweet old thing! What are you doing here in the Tangleroost? Did you follow me all the way from Deadwood just to git in my pants, you horny rascal?"

Longarm turned wearily to face the dumpy, plain-faced woman in pants by an open saloon entrance. He noticed they were being watched from inside. He sighed and said, "Howdy, Miss Calamity. How in thunder did you get down here from the Dakotas? I hope you didn't steal another stagecoach."

Calamity Jane Canary grinned like the overgrown tomboy she was and replied, "Hell, sweet loving man, there ain't a serious market hunter east or west of the Mississip' who ain't heard about the grand shooting contest they're holding here. I come down from Deadwood with both Deadwood Dicks and Sweet Sioux Yates, to git in on all that prize money. But don't worry, I arrived pure as ever, if you wants to camp with us. I've been saving my virginity for you alone, ever since they kilt my poor Wild Bill."

Longarm doubted that, but he knew that within the

hour anyone in town who hadn't already heard old Calamity bellow his real handle would no doubt be informed by the lady in person that her famous lover, Longarm, was in town. He'd never made love to her, any more than the late James Butler Hickock had, but he and old Calamity had ridden together against outlaws a spell back, so it wouldn't have been right to arrest her for disturbing his peace. He knew if he asked her not to tell anyone he was in town it would just make her brag about him harder and, worse yet, make her want to tag along. Old Calamity and her Deadwood drinking partners could be surprisingly good in a noisy showdown, but they just didn't have what it took for undercover investigation.

He said, "Well, since the damage has been done, you wouldn't know where I could find a gent called U. S. Marshal Moran, would you?"

Calamity Jane spat tobacco juice politely to one side of his boots and replied, "Sure I would. He's up to a hospital in Pine Bluff. One of his kids took sick sudden, so he had to go home. He left his chief deputy, a gent calt O'Carroll, in command here. You'll find him and the others in the back of the Western Union. You feds has took it over as a field headquarters."

"I thank you, Miss Calamity. But how come you know so much about the secrets of Uncle Sam these days? No offense, but we both know that story you give out about scouting for General Terry in the Black Hills don't seem to be on record with the War Department."

She looked hurt. "A lot *they* know! George Armstrong Custer told me personal there wasn't another scout for the U. S. Army as good as me. I knowed about Moran and company the same way everyone *else* in town right now knows it. It's pure common knowledge. I volunteered to help out when old Moran had to leave his juniors in command. But young O'Carroll just laughed at me. How come so many of you brutes laugh at me these days, Longarm? They didn't laugh at me when I was working for Madame Moustache in Dodge, right after the War. Cowhands used to *fight* over me, right after the War. I ain't changed all that much since then, have I?"

He assured her she still looked a lot like the fancy gal he'd admired in Dodge when the world had been younger. It was a lie, but at least it was a white one. It sure was amazing what a mere fifteen years of hard living and hard drinking could do to a once not-bad-looking woman. He thanked her for her information and said he'd likely see her around town again. As he turned away she bawled out loud enough to be heard all over a bigger town, "I'm holding you to that promise, Longarm! Come back to me by moonlight and I'll be proud to show you how a real woman treats an old friend!"

The back of Longarm's neck was still red as he turned into the Western Union, told the telegraph clerk on duty who he was and what he wanted, and was led into a back room.

The only man there was seated at a hauled-in picnic table and allowed as he was Deputy U. S. Marshal Sean O'Carroll. He was a good-looking young jasper with coal-black hair and an Irish brogue you could cut with a knife. He stood up to shake, poured Longarm a coffee cup of what he called "the Creature," even though it tasted more like corn liquor, and confirmed what Calamity had said about his superior, Marshal Moran, being called home by a family emergency. Longarm told him why the notion of working under cover had never been so hot in the first place, and O'Carroll told him just to dump his gear in a corner and work out of there with the rest of them if he wanted to.

Longarm waited until he'd stowed his possibles and sat down across the table from O'Carroll before he asked where all the other deputies were. The Irishman said, "Well now, thim four from the Pine Bluff office with me are out snooping in the swamp this minute, because Himself suspects some hunters drawn to this grand contest may have pointed guns at grander targets in other parts. You're the first of the outside help we sent for who's managed to get here."

Longarm nodded. "It wasn't as easy as Moran and Billy Vail might have figured it would be." He brought his fellow lawman up to date on his recent misadventures.

When he got to the poisoned tobacco, O'Carroll frowned. "Faith, that's odd. We just got a wire from Deputy Riggins of the Omaha office, saying he can't make it because of food poisoning! You don't suppose . . . ?"

But Longarm was already on his feet and on his way to the telegraph office out front. As O'Carroll joined him, somewhat confused, Longarm told the clerk, "I want to send a message to Marshal Moran in Pine Bluff. Tell him to tell his doctor to check his kid for a poison called henbane."

The telegrapher blanched and said he'd get right on it. As he commenced to tap out the wire to Pine Bluff, Longarm grabbed a pad and sat down to compose an all-points warning to other federal offices. It didn't take him long. As he rose again and placed it beside the telegraph key, O'Carroll frowned and said, "Wait a minute, Longarm. Moran's boyo is far too young to be after *smoking* poisoned anything!"

"Have you ever met a kid who wouldn't eat candy? The scientific gal who told me about henbane says it works sneaky, no matter how you mix it with your spit and swallow it. The sneaky part is that the effects creep up in a way few doctors would suspect right off as poison. Henbane just makes you sick and stupid till you either die in a way that looks natural or have some really wild dreams like I did."

O'Carroll nodded and said, "I fathom the fairy trick that was played on yourself, Longarm. But neither Moran's sick kid nor that other deputy who came down with something have been attacked by guns as well. How do you explain the shoot-out in K.C. as part of some grand plot against the government?"

Longarm shrugged. "I just added two and two to get three. Now that I think on it, it wouldn't make sense to sic a hired gun on a man you'd *poisoned!* Old Snake Simmons was just on the run, dressed at first like an ugly old woman, when he spotted me aboard the train from Denver. I didn't recognize him for two reasons. I hadn't seen the Wanted flier on him yet, and I really did take him for a mighty ugly old gal no man would look at more'n he had to. But Simmons had a suspicious nature and, in all modesty, I got a rep for being good at catching escaped killers. Snake didn't *know* I'd been slipped drugged cheroots. He thought I was just biding my time before I moved in on him. So he moved first and gunned the wrong berth by mistake. He must have shit when he found out I was still alive. He figured I'd penetrated his disguise. So he turned back into a gent. When we met again in the K.C. Depot dining room he must have shit again, figuring I'd trailed him there. Then, as he tried to make up his mind what to do next, he saw that I looked sick more than I was looking at him, and decided he'd never in this world get a better crack at me. He was right. But I told you about Miss Winslow saving my fool ass twice. I'd have likely gone on smoking poison had not she been so smart as well as dangerous!"

O'Carroll mulled it over some, then nodded and said, "Sure and it all hangs together. But you didn't die, that other deputy didn't die, and so far Moran's kid is still alive, sick as he might be. Don't that mean whoever's behind all this poison business might not be out to kill *anyone* all the way?"

Longarm started to object that poisoning anyone with henbane could hardly be called an act of kindness. Then he nodded. "Had I not met up with Tess, by now I'd likely be too sick and confused to be worth a damn to anyone, dead or alive. That other deputy ain't, and Moran *has* been put out of action for now, whether his son lives or not. Yeah, the sons of bitches are pretty smart. Even if we catch 'em, we can't nail 'em with murder one! I was sort of wondering about that. Why poison anyone with a tricky herb like henbane when strychnine would work cheaper as well as better? You can buy strychnine in any hardware store if you've been having coyote trouble, and it has no smell even a coyote's dainty nose can detect."

O'Carroll grimaced and said, "You may be curing me of smoking until we get to the bottom of this plot. You mentioned 'the plotters,' in the plural. How do you know it ain't *one* mad poisoner, Longarm?"

"Hell, that's the *easy* part. How could one maniac be in so many places at the same time? The three victims we know of for sure had to have been poisoned within the same rough cut of time, in Colorado, Nebraska, and Arkansas!"

"Aye. That adds up to at least *three* of the divvels!"

The telegrapher handed Longarm a message that had just come in from Fort Worth in answer to his all-points. He scanned it, swore, and handed it to O'Carroll as he muttered, "Make that four. The deputy Fort Worth was supposed to send just woke up from what they thought until now was an awesome drunk. I think we just saved him his job. But they don't have anyone else they can spare right now."

He left O'Carroll to figure out what the Arkansas office was going to do about being short-handed. He knew what *he* had to do. In the other room, he was changing into his rougher work clothes as the junior deputy rejoined him, saying, "Cheyenne, too. They thought their man had food poisoning when he returned so green-faced and covered with puke. Do you still think it was that gorl you met on the train who slipped you the doctored cheroots?"

Longarm buttoned his blue jeans. He shook his head and said, "The more I think on poor Penny Twinkles, the dumber I remember her. The people behind this are too smart to use feather-brained dancing girls. It might work once, but they couldn't count on all of us being stupid when a pretty gal bumps into us. I got to study on their method some before I can offer a sensible answer."

He put on a denim jacket over the hickory shirt and proceeded to strap his sixgun rig in place. The derringer and watch he usually packed in his tweed vest was now in one breast pocket of the short jacket. The smokes he'd bought in Fort Smith, sealed, were over his heart in the heavy shirt. O'Carroll got so exhausted watching him that he had to sit down for another cup of white lightning. Longarm put his Stetson back on, picked up his Winchester, and said, "Should anyone ask, I'll be out in the swamp, hunting."

But O'Carroll said, "Not so fast, damn it! Come and sit by my side if you love me and tell me what in the divvel's going on! I've only been in this country five years, and your Yankee customs continue to amaze me."

Longarm allowed he'd have some creature for the road, but as he perched on the corner of the table he said, "You know as much as I do. The only way to find out more is to go out and look. I doubt like hell anyone's about to come in here and sign a full confession in the next few minutes."

"Someone has to man this headquarters," O'Carroll insisted defensively as he poured. "Nothing about this case makes sense. The boyos working with us have yet to spot a wanted man in or about the town, and that can't be the motive of some mad master criminal in any case! If he meant to be after covering up for members of some gang, he'd only have to order thim to stay the hell *away* from here, right?"

Longarm clinked cups with him and agreed, "Moran was only expecting the prize money here to attract assorted and not-too-bright gunslicks, acting independent. A gang of serious crooks, working together, would have to be after something big as hell if they felt the need to poison the law all over Robin Hood's barn. Let's talk about the prize money. If they really mean to hand it out a thousand a day, starting *mañana,* the sooner someone steals it the more they'll have to steal."

O'Carroll shook his head. "Sure, that's the first thing Marshal Moran thought, before his boy took sick. Amalgamated Ammo means to pay by check. Their front man's over at the hotel, with the checkbook, of course. He told Moran his instructions are to make out each prize check to the winner of the day and thin sign it. Moran says anyone poaching a book of blank checks would be after baying at the moon for all the money he'd ever see."

"Ouch. Had my boss knowed that he'd likely never have sent me! Even a crook would have to be mighty stupid to enter a contest where he'd have to cash a check made out to him personal! Banks can be a mite picky when a total stranger named Smith or Jones comes in to cash a cool thousand with fuzzy I.D."

O'Carroll sipped white lightning thoughtfully and said, "I think Himself suspects something more crooked than Mister Jissy James in the flesh shooting ducks for paper he'd have a time turning into drinking money. Moran said the contest itself makes no sense at all, at all."

Longarm nodded and agreed. "Billy Vail said your boss was smart. I just come in through the flooded woods and I didn't see enough wild life to mention. That scientific gal I told you about opined it ain't good birding country, too. She said the swamps needed to strike a new balance of nature before it would be good. What do the locals say about the duck hunting hereabouts?"

The junior deputy looked blank. Longarm rose, saying, "Never you mind. I'll ask 'em. I'd best have a word with the front man from the ammo trust while I'm about it. You say he's at the hotel?"

"He is. His name would be Slade. And, one more thing—Moran's checked him out, and he didn't like what the Post Office had to say about him at all, at all."

"Do tell? What's old Slade been up to, when he ain't holding bird-shooting contests in piss-poor birding country?"

O'Carroll said, "Mail fraud. Before he went to work for the ammo thrust, Mr. Jacob Slade was selling a sure cure for baldness by mail order. Only, for some rason, nobody who sint the darling man a dollar iver got new hair, or innything else, from him!"

"What about the company he's working for now?"

"Moran's still gnawing that great bone. The Amalgamated Ammo whatever has a dacent credit rating, and

64

so far nobody's had a hard word to say about the goods they peddle. Mostly shotgun shells, according to their advertising."

"Bird shot, of course?"

"How'd you iver guess? That's supposed to be the whole point of this foolish contest. Me boss, as I told you, has his doubts."

Longarm nodded, put down his cup, and went on out to see how he felt about a situation that was sounding dumber by the minute.

Chapter 5

The scattered pattern of almost wet and almost dry made it a foolish notion to hire either a boat or a livery horse to explore the Tangleroost away from the railroad causeway. But Longarm could walk, if he had to, and it was getting late in the day to consider a serious expedition, in any case. He just wanted to get more of a feel about the fool country before he asked any more foolish questions about it.

He followed the tracks out the far side for perhaps a mile and wasn't astounded by anything he saw, smelled, or heard. This stretch of the Tangleroost looked and smelled as dead and rotten as the mess on the far side of town, and the occasional shotgun blast he heard from time to time added up to earlier arrivals cheating on the contest, as had been suggested. He wondered what they were shooting at. It sure seemed bleak and birdless in these parts. But there did seem to be a few patches of sedge grass or fiddlehead ferns spring sprouting among the mouldy tree trunks hither and yon as he got further from the settlement. It didn't smell as sour out this way, either. He spotted a path leading away from the tracks between puddles of oily water, so he dropped off the higher railroad bank to see where it might lead.

For openers, it led in too many directions to have been started by the feet of humankind. From the way it stayed dry by going the long way around even the slightest dip in the black leaf-mold, he judged it to be an old deer path, even though the flooded forest would hardly support deer worth mention, these days. He kept an eye on the sky as he wandered deeper into the swampland. With the branches above so naked, it would take a real greenhorn some time to get really lost out here. But he was glad the sky wasn't overcast. This was no place to spend even one night unintentionally.

The puddles he passed looked cleaner now and the floating patches of duckweed grew thicker and healthier. The path led through patches of waist-high sedge in places, and there were more fallen trees all around. He had to step over more than one and, when he did, he saw they were punky and going to mushrooms. He heard a door knock, looked up, and saw an ivory bill looking back down at him. He smiled up at the big old woodpecker and said, "You just go on about your chores, old son. I can see that silver maple's rotten as hell, too. This stretch has been dead longer and maples ain't as acid as oak, in the first place."

He moved on, wondering why this part of the swamp had obviously been under water longer. The story was that the Arkansas had lapped over its natural levee to flood the lower bottomlands beyond all at once. Yet even he could see that some parts had been drowned longer than others. He shrugged and moved on. The path led him into a patch of cattails and just gave out. Flood water had scoured through the old deer trail. As he took a few exploratory steps into the squishy reeds, he spied a bird's nest full of little blue eggs nestled in the cattails ahead, and gave up the notion. No bird would be dumb enough to build that low, where critters on legs could get at it. One of his socks was already commencing to squish inside its boot by the time he was back on firmer footing. He grimaced and said, "Nice try, Swamp. But I'll let you know when and if I ever mean to get *that* deep in you!"

He started back the way he had come, mulling over the little he'd seen so far. There *were* birds in the Tangleroost. There still weren't enough for it to be such a famous game reserve. He wondered why it seemed even deader near the tracks. Passing trains threw off sulfur-soured cinders and of course they used road tar, cut thin, to keep weeds from growing between the ties. But even the more serious lines cutting across the high plains to the west didn't cut that wide a swathe of destruction through the natural vegetation. There had to be another reason.

He heard an awesome roar off to his right and stiffened, looking up sudden lest it be a silver maple coming his way. Silver maple did that a lot, even when it was still alive. But it wasn't a shivered tree or even a lightning bolt from the blue he'd just heard. As the echoes faded away, he decided it had to be a punt gun. There was no mistaking the direction such a mighty bang had taken place, so he headed that way to see what could possibly call for so much powder and ball.

He had to leave the deer path to do it, of course, so both socks were squishing some by the time he climbed up on a fallen tree to spot about ten acres of oxbow lake ahead. On the far side, blue gunsmoke was still rising against the blackness of dead trees. He started to circle the little lake. It wasn't easy, and the swamp nearly got him more than once before he'd made it to the higher and dried ground on the far side. Moving through the deadwood, he spied what looked like two ragged-ass boys in an old gray ducking punt, poling shoreward, his way, through a mess of floating feathers. As the kid in the stern poled, the one in the bow was gathering in soggy dead ducks. It wasn't hard to fathom how they'd all died at once. The punt gun propped over the blunt bow was longer than the kid who'd just fired it, with at least a two-inch bore.

Longarm stepped into view at the shoreline as they slowly poled his way, too busy, at first, to notice him standing there. Each wore jeans and floppy-brimmed Ozark hats. The one in the bow had opened the front of his ragged gray shirt. That was how Longarm could see, even before he noticed the long hair, that the he was a she, and built mighty interesting as well.

The dishwater blonde in the bow spotted him about the same time he noticed what fine tits she had. She called out, "We got us a *gun*, here, mister!"

He called back, "So've I, Sis. But I come in peace. They call me Longarm, and I'm the law, not an escaped lunatic."

The one in the stern stopped poling and called out, "We ain't poaching, lawman. This here lake is *ourn!*"

He could tell by her voice that she was she-male, too, albeit dressed more sedate. He assured them he wasn't interested in their ducks or the unsporting way they'd just shot the same. So she poled closer to let her sidekick gather in more. By the time they had them all they were within easy talking distance and he could see they were both young and pretty, even though, between them, they didn't add up to intelligent enough to make a single schoolmarm worry about her job. The one in the stern was a brunette. They looked like sisters and, when he asked them about that, the blonde in the bow, who still hadn't bothered to button up, allowed they were the Halifax sisters, Luke and Lester. Luke was the blonde and Lester the brunette. He didn't comment on the names, but someone in the past must have, for Luke said, "Our Pa wanted boys. Our cabin's just down the lake, if you'd care for cake and coffee or sump'n."

The darker Lester giggled sort of dirty and added they served the best sump'n in the Tangleroost. Longarm had to study some on their offer. Then, as young Lester stood in the stern to pole better in the shallows, he wondered why on earth a healthy grown-up man would have to study on such a friendly offer. Even with her pants on, old Lester sure had nice legs. They both looked healthy, even if they could have used a little soap and water, and *he* was growing up more by the minute. So he said, "I'd best walk you ladies home, then. I come out here to see how much wildlife there might be in this mysterious swamp."

His life got wild as hell as soon as the Halifax sisters had led him to their one room tumbledown log cabin a few yards down the shore. The brunette told her sister to haul the ducks into the smokehouse out back, as she meant to put the kettle on for their honored guest. But the little blonde said, "Like hell I will! I seen him *first*, dear sister!"

Longarm laughed and said, "Hold on, ladies. Why don't *I* drag your bag to the smokehouse for you, while you both tend the stove inside?"

They exchanged thoughtful looks. He could tell it was an effort for either of them to think too hard. Then blonde

Luke nodded and said, "Just leave 'em sacked on the floor. I'll hang 'em to smoke later, once I'm feeling better."

He helped them drag the punt out and as Luke picked up the big bird blaster he saw she'd already sacked most of the ducks she'd gathered. Lester stuffed a few she'd missed in a fresh gunny and handed the sack to him as he gathered the first three. Four sacks of game and his Winchester made for an awkward load, but when she offered to help her sister sobbed that wasn't fair. Longarm said he could manage and the two of them literally scampered into the cabin.

He chuckled his way around to the smaller smokehouse, got the sloping door open, and tossed the sacks into the murky interior. It smelled like they were using shagbark for smoking. That was no mystery, in a swamp filled with dead trees. He shut the door and picked up his carbine to head back to the cabin. With any luck at all, he knew he'd get more than coffee and cake if he hung about until after dark and, thanks to his cautious approach to Miss Penny Twinkles and the cautious way Tess Winslow had been treating him ever since, he felt sure he'd be up to the task.

But when he stepped inside the cabin he saw that the Halifax gals hadn't put the coffee on just yet. They'd both taken off all their duds and were squatted on the dirt floor by a big four-poster bed that took up half the space inside. Luke grinned up at him and said, "I seen you first, but I'm a good sport. So we're aiming to play spin the bottle to see who goes first with you."

He said, "I can see you gals don't get many visitors. What was that about you having a daddy, though?"

Luke said, "Shoot, he died over a year ago, and Ma

71

died when we was little." Then she said, "Hot damn, I win! How come you still got your duds on, handsome stranger? Are you a sissy?"

He laughed, allowed he wouldn't want any gals as pretty as them to consider him a sissy, and shucked his own denims fast to back his brag. The next few minutes were sort of confusing. They both jumped on the bed ahead of him and he'd thought they'd all agreed he was meant to mount the blonde first. But though he was willing and she acted downright anxious, her brunette sister was all over him, too.

Normally, Longarm let it soak polite in a gal while they pondered their next move after coming the first time. But the horny little brunette dragged him off the blonde, rolled him on his back, and forked a firm thigh across him. She started bouncing atop him like a jockey racing for the home stretch, sobbing with passion.

The blonde he'd just had rolled over, groped for the bottle on the floor by the bed, and yanked the cork with her teeth before she said, "This calls for a drink."

He took a swallow of corn from the bottle Luke offered, shut his eyes tight so they wouldn't water, and gasped, "Wow, that sure is good stuff. You make it yourselves?"

Luke shook her blonde head and said, "Can't. Corn don't grow for miles no more. We git it offen the Grannywitch, over near the edges where she has her still. Leastways, it *used* to be the edges. The Tangleroost gits bigger all the time."

Lester said, "That's the pure truth. When we was little our lake lay smack in the middle of pretty green woods. I sure miss the way it was. Daddy had his own corn patch and garden out back. Now we has to buy grits to go with the game we shoot. Grits goes good with duck, but ever' year about this time I recalls the fresh greens we used to fry with meat. Grits don't go worth a hang with fish, you know. I sure would admire some okra fried with catfish, right now."

"You catch many fish in that lake outside, Lester?"

"Some. Why else would Daddy have run off with Ma to this clearing, if the hunting and fishing had been poorly?"

Luke swallowed more corn, wheezed, and added, "It used to be lots better out here, afore the boils ruint ever'thing."

"Boils?" asked Longarm cautiously, propping himself up on one elbow to look them both over more carefully. He saw that the naked bodies in bed with his were unblemished, if tanner and somewhat less perfumed than high fashion called for in other parts. Luke went on, "The Grannywitch knows more about the boils than we does, living closer to 'em. She says water boiling up outten the ground accounts for all the infernal water around here. Some army men come by a few years back to see if there was some way to git the water to stay in the durned old Arkansas betwixt floods, but they gave up when they seen them boils."

Lester snuggled closer to him from the other side and pouted, "I sure wish the land hereabouts didn't have boils. It used to be so nice in the Tangleroost."

"Mostly hardwood forest as only flooded once or twice a year, eh?" Longarm asked.

"Yep, just enough to green things up. Our daddy said trees growed gooder if they got flooded and then got to dry out. He knowed ever'thing about living in the woods. He'd been living in 'em regular ever since he kilt a man in the Ozarks afore we was birthed."

Longarm nodded. He'd heard the story before, he

73

suspected. But he was a little shocked just the same when Luke volunteered, "It was over Ma. The preacher man where they growed up in the hills said it was wrong for them to live together as man and wife. He said he aimed to take 'em to the law about it. So Pa kilt the son of a bitch and they run off to live happily ever after in the woods. At least, they did till Ma caught the ague and died on us. The Grannywitch says it was on account of how damp the Tangleroost got, after we'd lived here a spell."

As the three of them shared a smoke, with a blond head on one of his shoulders and a darker one on the other, Longarm asked, "Could you gals show me the way to this Grannywitch woman? How far off in the swamp does she live?"

Luke said, "Too fur to make it by sundown, and it ain't safe after dark. There's haunts around her cabin. What do you want with the Grannywitch, anyways? She's old and ugly and an Injun besides."

"No, she ain't," Lester said. "Pa said she was a nigger. Half leastways. She run off to the woods when they still kept slaves. Back when the Tangleroost was still woods instead of a swamp."

"A lot you know," Luke said. "The Grannywitch tolt me her own self she was half Natchez. She hid out in the woods when the army said her kin had to move out West to the great desert."

"Shoot, she just made that up."

Luke didn't answer. She was kissing her way down Longarm's naked flank. He groaned and said, "No fooling, gals, I ain't sure I'm up to any more right now."

But the blonde persisted in her perversion and, after a while, he discovered he wasn't as used up as he'd

74

thought he might be. By the time he got away it was getting dark and he had one hell of a time finding his way back to town.

Chapter 6

He limped first to the Western Union to see if there was any fresh news. Marshal Moran had wired that his son was out of danger and he would be returning directly. In the back, O'Carroll had been rejoined by his fellow deputies. They were introduced to Longarm as Deputies Doyle, Mahoney, Fagin, and Ryan. Longarm knew half the Indian-fighting army was Irish these days, since few native-born Americans wanted to serve for thirteen dollars a month when a cowhand could earn a dollar a day. But it still seemed to him that Moran might be overdoing it a bit. O'Carroll was the only one who'd been in the States for over a year. Three of them had such heavy brogues they were hard to understand and Fagin, a little guy who looked like he'd been born under a mushroom, spoke so little English that the others had to translate some of the words for him. He noticed they all spoke the Gaelic if they had to. He wondered if they bothered with English at all when they were alone together.

The four who'd been out in the swamp that afternoon hadn't seen anything interesting. Fagin, who would seem to have been a poacher in his native land, opined that the Tangleroost was a terrible place to be holding a shootoff. Longarm didn't want to argue the point, even if it hadn't looked like so much work. He leaned his Winchester in the corner by his possibles and turned around again to say, "I heard today about some sort of speywoman who's been living in this neck of the woods since they was still woods. She's called the Grannywitch. Any of you boys heard the locals speaking of her?"

The five Irishmen looked blank. Mahoney made the sign of the cross and said, "A witch would account for a lot indaid! Them's *thurribble* woods out there, Longarm. Why do ye suppose them gints from Chicago picked it for a hunt at all, at all?"

"Your boss, Marshal Moran, would like to know that, too. I'm going over to the hotel now to see if that front man for the ammo trust has any notion what he's doing here. Any of you want to come along?"

They all looked dubious. O'Carroll said, "Himself told us not to mix with thim boyos in the saloon next door till he got back."

Ryan nodded and said, "That's the thruth of it. For some rason we seem to strike thim Ozark ruffians as funny, and we don't fancy being laughed at."

Doyle nodded silently and cracked his knuckles morosely. Longarm nodded and went out again alone.

He tried the hotel first. A different clerk on duty said Slade wasn't in his room upstairs and suggested the saloon next door. Longarm said he'd do that, forgiving Moran's green crew for lacking interest in the local night life even before he reached the swinging doors. There was nothing else going on in the dinky jerkwater at this hour, so the one saloon was attempting to sound like all of Dodge on a Saturday night.

It was almost as crowded. There was no sense asking anyone to excuse you if you wanted to get to the bar. You just had to shove. He was sure some of the men he shoved out of his way would have fallen down dead drunk in less crowded surroundings. A few gave him dirty looks and asked who he thought he was shoving. But it was too tightly packed to enjoy even a knife fight, so he just smiled and kept going.

Most of the crowd wore the same wool hats the Halifax sisters fancied. But he spied hats with Texas peaks, Colorado crushes, Wyoming dimples, and so forth. Some wore old army hats, and there were pug hats and derbies enough to indicate hunters from all over creation had come for the big shootoff, starting in the morning. He didn't see any faces worth arresting for anything more serious than drunk and disorderly, though. He wondered just what in the hell Marshal Moran had left out of those wires to the other offices. The only thing that made sense was unethical. It wasn't any other marshal's fault if Moran had recruited a mess of green shamrocks who might not recognize Jesse James or The Kid on sight. Each office was supposed to hire experienced lawmen, not borrow them from others when they were needed.

He finally got to the bar, where a fat gal in a too-tight red satin dress made room for him, called him "lover," and asked if he wanted to buy her a drink first or just take her up to the cribs and get down to business. Her hair was a lot blonder than Luke's had been. A lot more artificial, too. But he favored her with a wistful smile and told her, "Mayhaps another time, ma'am. Right now I'm here on business. I'm looking for a gent called Slade."

She shrugged her bare shoulders and said, "In the back room, dealing stud, Stud. You sure you ain't got time? I admire your clean smell as well as them shoul-

78

ders. I can tell when a man's just had a bath, and you've no idea what a refreshing change that can be in a place like this."

He nodded understandingly down at her and said, "I just had a swim and used some naphtha soap whilst I was at it. By the way, do you know anything about boils in the swamps all around?"

She sniffed and said, "Look, if you don't want me you can just say so, damn it. You don't have to get insulting about it!"

He saw he would have to word inquiries about the witch woman's mysterious boils more delicately in the future. Maybe they'd sound better as springs, even if they likely were leaks under the levee.

It only took forever to shove his way to the rear of the crowded saloon. The usual big moose was standing with his back to the usual door and, as usual, he told Longarm, "You can't go in there."

Longarm smiled and said, "Sure I can. You just have to get the hell out of my way, sonny."

The saloon tough smiled fondly at Longarm. "I'm sure pleased to see this ain't gonna be such a boring evening after all. I generally don't get to kick the shit out of anyone this side of midnight. But just hold still and I promise you won't feel a thing."

Longarm laughed and said, "Your offer sure is tempting. For a man has to do *something* before bedtime, and up to now I ain't been tempted by the other pleasures of this clip joint. But I wouldn't want to stomp your ugly head before I'd introduced myself."

"Shit, I don't care who you might be, pilgrim. I'm Fisheyes Brown, and I eat little boys like you for breakfast. So name your pleasure. Fist city, or do you really want to tempt fate? I notice you're packing a pissy little

79

Colt. I eats Colts for breakfast, too."

"It's been fun jawing with you, Fisheyes. But I'm law, they call me Longarm, and one way or another I'm going through that door behind you."

The big bullboy blanched and got out of the way quickly, asking, "Can't you tell when a man's just funning, Mr. Longarm?"

Longarm assured Fisheyes of his continued friendship and went on in. Six or eight men were standing around a table in the center of the back room. Four men were seated at the same, staring poker-faced at one another across an awesome pot, which was only fair. The fancy gal had said they were playing stud poker back here.

A hatchet-faced individual with eyes like snakes glanced up from the cards he was dealing to tell Longarm flatly, "Get out of here, cowboy. This is a private game."

Longarm nodded pleasantly and asked if he was Jacob Slade. The mean-eyed dealer said, "No. I'm Steamboat Palmer. Name mean anything to you, cowboy?"

Longarm answered, "Yep. You're supposed to be a mighty dangerous man to cross."

Palmer said, "I am. More so when I'm playing cards. So do yourself a favor and *git,* while you can."

Longarm ignored the threat to ask, "Which one of you is Slade?"

A weaker-chinned fat man in a checkered suit held up his pale hand timidly, like a kid asking the teacher if he could go take a leak. Longarm smiled down at him and said, "I'm Deputy U. S. Marshal Long, and I'd like a word with you in private, Mr. Slade."

Slade smiled and started to rise, gathering his own winnings together. The tinhorn dealing snapped, "Sit down, you fat bastard. Nobody leaves the table when I'm dealing."

Slade gulped and murmured, "Mr. Palmer, the man says he's the *law!*"

Steamboat Palmer glanced coldly up at Longarm, shrugged, and said, "I don't care if he's Jesus Christ himself. I'll tell you when this game is over. Shut up and let me deal."

Longarm asked politely, "Mr. Slade, are you ready to leave the table?"

Slade was too scared to answer. Longarm knew there wasn't much he could do about it unless a citizen out and out requested the protection of the law. Gambling wasn't a federal offense, and a man could even get away with scaring folk, if he worded it right. Palmer sneered up at Longarm and asked, "Do you have a search warrant signed by a local judge, oh famous one?"

Longarm sighed. "Not hardly."

Palmer said, "Get out of here, then. I own this joint. You're on my private property, and under common law I have the right to shoot you as a trespasser, you know."

For some reason, that made all the other gents standing about the table edge out of the way. Longarm chuckled fondly. "It's one thing to say and another to do, Steamboat. What makes you so ornery this evening? Are you afeared an old country boy like me might pay attention to them lily-white hands as you're dealing to your suckers?"

Slade murmured, "Long, for God's sake!"

Everyone else in the room stopped breathing for a spell.

Steamboat Palmer slowly rose from his seat, throwing open his black frock coat to expose the grips of his two ivory-mounted pistols as he asked ominously, "Are you accusing me of cheating these other gents, Longarm?"

Longarm said, "Just two of 'em. The one sitting next to Slade has to be your confederate. He's the only one with his hands out of sight, and if he knows what's good for him he'll just leave his belly gun where it is and place both hands on the table, polite."

The tinhorn indicated slowly placed his hands flat on the table as Steamboat Palmer rasped, "Not that way, stupid!" and made an awful mistake with his own hands, likely without thinking ahead too clearly.

When the smoke cleared, Longarm was still on his feet, and the late Steamboat Palmer lay sprawled against the far wall with his guns still holstered and three smoking holes in his vest that had never been there before.

Someone was pounding on the door behind Longarm, but Longarm had locked it behind him on entering. He said, "I still got two rounds in this Colt and a derringer you'll just have to guess about. Am I correct in assuming you with the pearl-gray hat and pinky ring was the junior partner of this firm?"

The confederate froze with his palms flat on the table, gulped, and said, "It wasn't my idea, Longarm. I never thought Steamboat would go up agin a man of your rep. He's been sniffing some sort of white powder up his nose of late and, to tell the truth, I was scared he'd kill *me* any minute!"

"You got a name, friend?"

"They calls me the Saint Joe Kid. You was right about us being partners, but I swear I meant you no serious injury!"

Longarm nodded. "I've heard of you. Up until now you've just been a punk card sharp. Now, if we word things right, you may be the owner of this whole setup. So what's it going to be?"

"Anything you say, Longarm!"

"All right. I'm saying I come in here peacable to meet Mr. Slade, here. I'm saying, and you're saying, that asshole on the floor drawed on me and got shot in self-defense."

The Saint Joe Kid said that was the simple truth, and nobody else in the room wanted to debate him. Longarm said, "Since you're the boss here, now, Kid, I'll assume you'll know how to deal with the remains and explain the new situation to your new hired help. If you send any after me, they'd best be good. For if they try and fail I'll be coming back and Lord knows *who's* likely to wind up owning this profitable business!"

The Saint Joe Kid said he'd always wanted to own his own saloon and whorehouse, and that he was much obliged to Longarm for allowing him to rise so fast in his profession.

Longarm told Slade to gather up his winnings and follow him. Slade said he never argued with a man with a gun. Longarm told everyone else to stay put until he and the front man had cleared the premises. Then he unlocked the door. When Fisheyes burst in, Longarm told the thug his new boss would explain, and led Slade out. For some reason, it was a lot easier to move across the saloon now. As the two of them stepped out on the plank walk, Longarm paused to reload. Then he suggested they go next door to the hotel lobby, where they could talk more privately.

They'd almost made it when Longarm heard a voice behind him shouting, "No, don't!" and turned to see Fisheyes bearing down on them with a wild look in his eyes and a gun in each fist.

Longarm shoved Slade to one side as he crabbed to the other, slapping leather. For a man starting out with the drop on his intended victim, Fisheyes was a better bouncer than a gunslinger. He missed twice, and then Longarm hit once, and that was the end of old Fisheyes.

The Saint Joe Kid bawled out from the distance, "I *never*, Longarm! I told him not to go after you, but he was sort of fond of the old boss and I just couldn't stop him!"

Longarm called back, "You're forgiven, this one last time. But for your sake, I sure hope that's the end of it!"

The Kid assured him from afar that it was, not daring to come any closer. Longarm heard boot heels coming the other way and turned to see all five of Moran's deputies charging his way, guns drawn. He called out, "Don't get your bowels in an uproar, boys. It's over, I hope."

As O'Carroll joined him above the body stretched like a bear rug on the plank walk, he asked about it anyway. Longarm explained in a few terse sentences. Then he asked, "Where were you all during my *first* shootout, a good five minutes back?"

"Sure, were thim other shots you, too? We hord thim, but thought nothing of it till we heard more gunshots, closer. Faith, guns have been going off all day around here, Longarm."

"I noticed. I'd be obliged if you'd take charge of the street, here, till whoever they got here as coroner shows up. Mr. Slade and me will be inside if I'm needed."

O'Carroll frowned thoughtfully. "Sure, and who do you think you are to be after giving us orders, Longarm? We work for Marshal Moran, not you!"

There was a Gaelic growl of agreement from the other four. Longarm said, "All right, *don't* take charge here. I don't give a shit. Come on, Slade."

They went inside. Slade asked if they wouldn't be safer talking upstairs in his room. Longarm glanced at the plate-glass window and agreed it might be more comfortable. Slade led him up to a corner room on the second floor. Longarm told him to leave the oil lamp unlit as he opened the blinds, glanced down at the now crowded street, and said, "There's plenty of light if we don't want to read any fine print. Sit down. We got some fine-print talking to do."

Slade sat on his bed. Longarm stayed by the window, reloading by the lamplight from outside. He decided to risk walking about with all six chambers loaded for now. He reholstered his .44 and said, "First question: was you gambling with your own money or your company's just now?"

Slade looked sheepish and replied, "My own, of course. The spot you got me out of just in time might have been occasioned by the fact they knew I was the field representative for Amalgamated. I told them I had no power to write company checks on my own, but old Steamboat said he was sure we could work something out if I lost."

"Hell, did you expect to *win?*"

"The thought that I might be in trouble had occurred to me just before you showed up to save my ass. That Steamboat sure was an unreasonable cuss."

"So he seemed to me as well. That's over for now. Next question: why the hell did you pick this Tangleroost as the site of your big shootout?"

Slade sighed and said, "I never. The board of directors up in Chicago picked it off the map. Betwixt rivers and railroads, St. Louis is the easiest place to get to from the rest of the country. But who ever heard of a bird-shooting contest in St. Lou? Someone said this delta country looked like a natural duck pond, it was called a tangle *roost,* and not all that far down from St. Lou. So here I am, and where are the goddamn ducks?"

"I saw a robin's nest this afternoon. What happens come morning, when your contest opens officially, if there ain't good shooting?"

Slade shrugged and said, "My instructions are to award the day's prize to whoever bags the most birds, of course."

"Do tell? I know some local gals who bagged four gunnies of ducks, recent. That ain't impressive by market-hunter standards, and I'm sure they nailed every duck on their lake. Could they win the grand prize for a mere four sacks of game?"

"Sure, if they've entered the contest and no other entrant comes in with five. Amalgamated Ammo don't give a shit about the birds themselves, Longarm. They just want to get famous as the sponsers of the contest, see?"

"You mean if some rascal come in with, say, one duck and nobody else got any all that day, he'd win a thousand dollars?"

"If nobody flushed duck one and he brought me a *bluebird* it'd be all the same to me. I was told to award a thousand a day for the best day's bag. Nobody said nothing about how many birds that'd have to be."

"It does have to be a critter with wings, though?"

"Oh, sure, we have to set *some* standards. Why are you so interested? Would you like an entry form? I've still got a few."

He started to rise. Longarm waved him back down and said, "I ain't here to shoot birds. I'm still trying to figure out what I *am* doing here, and how come someone's gone to so much trouble to prevent me and other experienced lawmen from witnessing a fool affair that, no offense, sounds more stupid than profitable. Are you sure you ain't packing any serious cash?"

Slade said, "Well, the hundred and eight dollars I won tonight thanks to you seems serious enough to me. I got another two-fifty of my own, and this hotel says it'll take my expense account checks. Before you ask, I can't draw more than twenty a day on my expense account."

Longarm thought. "Hmm, that's another two hundred worth of blank checks, if there was an easy way to cash checks after they was stolen. Do you have a list of all the shootists who've entered so far?"

Slade rose, went to the dresser, and produced a thick notebook, asking if Longarm wanted to see his checkbook and company promotion literature as well. Longarm grimaced and said, "Hell, I ain't got time to even go through that awesome entry list right now. But save it for me. You never know when it comes to paperwork. Can you offer me a rough estimate on how many contestants we're talking about, pard?"

Slade could do better than that. He turned to the last page and, squinting in the gloom, said, "One thousand, four hundred and forty-eight. I number each entry blank. These are the carbon copies. At the end of each shoot-out day I don't even look at a dead duck unless the gent making the claim can produce his entry form as well."

"That makes sense. But how in the hell can this bitty jerkwater hold that many folks at once? I doubt if there could be a thousand in town right now, and it's already crowded as hell."

"I've run contests before," Slade said. "A lot of them ain't here yet, and some who are must be camping out in the woods. Boys who hunt for a living ain't too welcome in hotels, even if they have the money. The other judges haven't arrived yet, save for Parson Moore, the local big shot we always like to have on the panel if we can. He'd be over to the Church of Eternal Salvation if you want to question him about the contest."

"Does he know anything about the contest?"

"No more than I just told you. Like I said, we invite locals to join the panel if they're willing. Most ain't, since we don't pay them more than the honor. But when we can get us such a sucker, it does make the contest seem more honest."

"What do you mean *seem* more honest? Who are the other judges you'll have helping you hand out all that money, Slade?"

The front man gulped nervously. "Couple of company men like me, a retired army man, and a couple of out-of-work political hacks from Pine Bluff. The contest *will* be honest, Longarm. Sore losers always wonder about such matters, but there's no way to rig a bird migration, and the company don't give two hoots in hell who wins. They already writ the whole ten thousand off as advertising."

"How come? Seems to me you could print a lot of brags in a lot of papers for less'n ten thousand whole dollars!"

Slade sighed. "Look, let's not try to fool one another. I know you're federal and I know what the Post Office says about my misspent youth. But if you won't take my word, ask any newspaper man you do trust if a country-wide coverage of a great shootoff, free, ain't worth the modest investment."

"I mean to. I drink regular with the Denver *Post*. What if your big shootoff turns out to be a big bust? I have it on good authority that this Tangleroost is about the worst place you could have chosen. There ain't much food and the dead trees all about screen such open water as there is. What if, come the next ten days, you don't bag enough birds to matter? Won't them same papers laugh at you fit to bust?"

Slade grinned in the gloom and said, "Of course. That'd be worth a million in publicity as well. Don't you get it yet? We don't *care* if the contestants down a million

88

birds or none at all. Either way, the papers will all carry *some* damned story about Amalgamated Ammo! You can admire Remington or Colt or you can make up jokes about 'em, but you know they sell guns and ammo. Amalgamated Ammo wants the same crack at the market. When a man goes into a store to buy something, he just says the first brand name that pops into his mind, see? My job is to make Amalgamated Ammo famous, not to enrich unwashed market hunters. And, hell, I *like* birds!"

Longarm laughed. "Unless this spring's migration has started late, the birds ain't in all that much trouble around here. I reckon I buy your story. It sounds too dumb for a real sneak to make up."

Chapter 7

They shook on it and parted friendly. So Longarm was alone in the dark hallway when he heard a woman whisper his name from a dark doorway and a manicured finger beckoned him inside on the double.

To his mild surprise, it wasn't Tess Winslow. But he wasn't too upset. The total-stranger-gal was pretty, had let down a mess of red hair for the night, as far as he could tell in the dim light, and didn't seem to notice that her silk kimono was open down the front a mite more than it should have been for greeting strange company. She said, "I'm Sylvia Norris. I'm Royal."

He stared down uncertainly and replied, "Do tell? I'm just a plain old U. S. citizen, Your Royalness."

She laughed. "I meant I'm with the Royal Society, you nit! I'm here to study the continental flow pattern of North American waterfowl, and all that rot."

He nodded in sudden understanding. "Oh, Canada geese must be British subjects part of the time, too. I'm sorry I'm so dumb tonight, Miss Sylvia. I just had two shootouts and, to tell the truth, I thought you was somebody else when I come in just now."

She moved over to her bed, sat down, and patted the covers at her side. "I heard about the gunplay. That window opens on the street. I saw you arrive with that Tess Winslow, earlier, as well. What did she tell you about me, Longarm?"

He remained standing to reply, "Nothing. I don't recollect her even mentioning the Royal Society. Are you all working with the Smithsonian on birds?"

She wrinkled her nose and said, "Hardly. I believe your Tess is camped with her bloody friends in a tent somewhere. I had the good sense to reserve this room well in advance. Don't you want to sit down?"

He sighed wistfully. "Want to. Can't. I got to get on down and find out if this township has a coroner and, if so, what he has to say about my recent misadventures."

She saw his hand reach for the knob. She rose again and let him smell some more perfume and see more of where it came from as she asked, "Would you come back when you're done? I have so much I want to talk to you about, Longarm."

"I'll come back if it ain't too late," he said, "and my friends call me Custis."

"I'll be waiting, Custis, no matter how late you want to come," she said.

By the time he got back downstairs he had decided he must have taken that last remark dirtier than intended. Gals that good-looking were seldom desperate. He found Deputy O'Carroll waiting for him in the lobby. The handsome young Irishman told him that the local coroner's jury was set up in the church down the tracks. As they headed for it together, O'Carroll said, "Sure and I may have been out of line a few minutes ago, but never give a Mayo man a direct order in front of his friends without giving him time to think about it."

Longarm nodded soberly. "Having to gun two men in less'n five minutes may have made *me* a mite terse, too. Let's call it a draw. I wasn't expecting the second one at all. I thought old Fisheyes and me had agreed he was sensible. What can you tell me about the coroner I'm going up against, Sean?"

O'Carroll said, "His name's Swanson. He's section boss for the railroad, in charge of the water tower, track repair, and all, and all. He acts as town coroner, mayor, or jist about anything he might want to, since most of the people left here since the grand flood work for him. He's all right, for a damned Protestant."

"Who acts as the local law?"

"Us. They wired for federal help when the town constable quit just as the big shootoff was announced. That was one of the things Marshal Moran found so fishy. He ordered us to bring the man and his deputies in for questioning, but none of thim seem to live here any more. I have their names at our field office, if you'd like to look thim over."

Longarm shrugged and said, "Later, mayhaps. Ain't much sense in trying to talk to gents who just ain't there. Naturally, nobody who still lives here can offer à suggestion as to why they lit out so unexpected?"

"No, but I have me own suggestion," O'Carroll said. "Moran thinks I may be overimaginative, though."

"Tell me what you imagine, Irish."

"Well, ain't it a fact some of your Yankee gunmen have been known to hire out as lawmen when they was resting up between train robberies?"

"Sure. Your countryman, Billy the Kid, once packed a deputy's badge for a spell. He had to give it back when he shot folk out of season. I follow your drift, and I admire your imagination. A vacationing outlaw *might*

92

find it sort of upsetting to learn that a whole mess of strangers from all over the country was about to visit his backwoods home away from home."

They walked on a few silent moments before Longarm added, "Damn. We ain't all that far from Clay County, and nobody's seen much of the James–Younger gang since the Northfield bank job went all wrong for 'em! Does that list you have include descriptions, Sean?"

The Irishman shook his head and replied, "No, just the names. Smith, Jones, and other English names an Irishman finds hard to remember. Marshal Moran found it curious none of thim had wives or even gorl friends anyone here in town knew of. But he said it was wrong to jump at asey conclusions."

Longarm grinned sheepishly. "He was right. I've been led down many a wrong path, following my first fool notion. But I'll keep yours in mind, just the same, for I can't come up with an easier reason for five gents to leave an easy job all at once. Usually, when the boss quits, his second-in-command gets his job by default. You'd think at least one of the deputies would have had some ambition."

They got to the end of the business block, swung the corner, and saw a white frame church—or a white barn with a bitty steeple on it—gleaming in the moonlight. The front door was open and a lamp was burning inside. It still looked sort of spooky, grinning at them like a big old skull against the brooding darkness of the Tangle-roost's dead trees.

Inside it was more cheerful, albeit bleak. The Church of Eternal Salvation was one of those bleak little backwoods cults that seemed to spring up where there was more corn liquor than book learning. They had shoved the benches out of the way and set up a long table in front of the plain pine pulpet. A row of gents were seated on the far side of the table. Longarm assumed the one chair facing them was meant for him. He still waited until the middle-aged gent in the middle smiled and told him to sit in it.

Coroner Swanson introduced the other members of his panel. The only one Longarm found even mildly interesting was a tight-lipped old fellow in rusty black to Swanson's right. Longarm disliked Parson Moore on sight, but that seemed fair, since he could see the feeling was mutual.

Swanson smiled more friendly and said, "This won't take but a minute, Deputy Long. Everyone else we've talked to seems to agree the rascals you had to shoot this evening died by pure, dumb misadventure. But we got to preserve the formalities."

Swanson leaned forward to hand Longarm a page of ruled yellow foolscap covered with neat handwriting. "Just look that over and sign next to that X at the bottom if you agree with it."

Longarm read it. He saw that it was supposed to be his own sworn statement. That struck him as a mite hasty, but they had him saying just about what he would have said under oath if he'd been a mite more boastful. So he accepted the offered pen and gave them his signature. He noticed that the "witnesses" to his sworn statement had already signed it. As he handed it back, the part-time coroner said, "That's settled, then. The township will bury the two rascals at their own expense and hold what's left over for thirty days for such kin as may come forward to claim it. At that time, we can vote on what's to be done with the money."

"Hold on," Longarm said. "Common law says you got to hold intestate funds longer than that, gents. You're supposed to advertise in the papers for possible heirs, and *ninety* days, not thirty, is the least you can offer, starting from the first day the notice is published."

A couple of the nonentities on the panel cursed. Swanson just looked hurt. "No shit? Well, we do want to do things proper. I'm surprised you seem to be so thoughtful about men you just blowed to kingdom come, Longarm."

Longarm shrugged and said, "I never shot neither, personal, and the heirs of skunks has rights just like anyone else. Wouldn't the junior partner of the late Steamboat Palmer be helpful in locating any kin left over?"

Swanson wrinkled his nose. "If you're talking about the Saint Joe Kid, we ordered him to leave town a few minutes ago," he said. "If he knows what's good for him, he won't get off the repair train I just put him on until it reaches the next section."

Longarm frowned thoughtfully, trying to figure the time since he'd heard that dinky whistle from up in Slade's room but ignored it as unimportant at the time. "I sure wish things was done less hasty around here," he said. "I wanted a word with that boy. I've a sneaking suspicion old Fisheyes Brown would not have come after me so wild, had he not been *ordered* to. Who might own the saloon and such, now that Steamboat's partner has vacated the premises so sudden?"

"Us, I reckon," Swanson said. "Steamboat may have overstated the case if he told you he owned it. He leased the property from the Tangleroost Holding Company. Him and his riffraff just moved in a few days ago, and now they're gone. I reckon we'll have to appoint a committee or something to run the operation while the big shooting contest is going on. After it's over, the whores and the tinhorns will likely be moving on, alas."

Parson Moore spat, "I demand we close that den of thieves and harlots at once! I told you all not to lease that property to such a depraved crowd in the first place!"

Swanson looked weary as he replied, "You're outvoted, Parson. I don't hold with sinning all that much, myself, but business is business, and Lord knows there ain't been much of *that* around here since the flood your same Lord chose to send us."

"Don't carry on so, Parson," another man on the jury said. "It ain't like our *own* folk are getting drunk and sinsome in that old saloon. It's better for our own wives and daughters if all them roughnecks from the outside world have a place to let off steam, see?"

Parson Moore grimaced. "Bah, you make me sick! Our Lord told the woman taken in adultery to go and sin no more, not to make sure she only did it with strangers!"

Longarm decided he liked the parson better after all. At least he didn't seem a *total* small-town hypocrite. But, as Swanson said, he was outvoted, and there was much to be said for the opposing view as well. Longarm wasn't, in fact, too sure the whores on hand would protect the local home gals all that well when the town got really crowded. But that wasn't his problem. He never would have held the contest in such a dumb place to begin with.

Chair legs commenced to scrape, and it looked like the meeting was about over. But as long as he had the local powers handy in one place, Longarm said, "Hold on, gents. I still got a few things to ask."

Swanson settled down again, but said, "Damn it, Longarm, we just *cleared* you. What else is there to be settled?"

"I'm a mite confused about this land-holding setup," Longarm said. "Slade said he had to lease the shooting

96

grounds off someone, and hardly anyone's left out in that dead swamp. Are you the gents he did business with?"

Swanson nodded, openly enough. "Us and the railroad," he explained. "The railroad holds title to a hundred feet on either side of their causeway. I run this section for them, but I had nothing to say about the contest when Slade got them to agree to it. The bottomlands all around, as you must have guessed, used to be held freehold by local settlers, woodcutters and such. As the rising waters drove people out, us businessmen in town formed a holding company to buy up the titles of abandoned land."

"For lots of money, no doubt?"

"You'd be surprised how cheap a flooded woodlot can be bought. We gave each owner a modest grubstake, though. We didn't want to cheat anybody."

"How come?" asked Longarm, poker-faced.

Swanson looked puzzled and asked, "Do you mean how come we took advantage of flooded-out nesters, or how come we wanted their useless land in the first place?"

Longarm said, "Both."

Swanson grinned and replied, "It's no great secret. The boys and me had two main motives. One was pure Christian charity, whether you believe it or not. Most of the poor trash whites was flat busted by the time they gave up trying to grow corn and truck under water."

"What's the more sensible reason, Swanson?"

"Greed, of course. A chance to make a future fortune from a mighty modest investment. The timber's worthless, rotting in muck too wet for logging, and there ain't no market for skunk cabbage and cattails. But the army engineers tell us there's an outside chance the whole township could be drained again. They say it's still a few feet above the Arkansas, save in flood time, and that floodgates punched through the levee would do the job if it wasn't for underground channels they just gave up on after a spell of trying to figure."

Longarm mulled that over, nodded grudgingly, and said, "I heard much the same tale, earlier. I reckon I'd best have a look at the so-called boils out in the middle of the swamp. What should I know in advance about the spey woman who's said to dwell by said boils?"

There was an uneasy muttering up and down the table. Parson Moore said, "I know of the dark slut, and the Good Book tells us, Thou shalt not suffer a witch to live!"

Swanson shot the preacher a disgusted look, but told Longarm, "Some say the Grannywitch is a gal it ain't safe to visit alone. She used to scare kids a lot, afore they moved away. If she offers you moonshine, don't drink it. One of them army engineers did, just afore he come down with swamp fever, they thought, and decided the survey just wasn't worth it."

"I'll keep that in mind," Longarm said. "I sure don't enjoy getting poisoned with herbs. But how in thunder do I get out to your old Grannywitch?"

Another juror said, "She ain't mine. But I got a boy who can guide you there. He's a nigger, too, so he ain't scared of the Grannywitch. I'm Hank Thorp. I run the livery stable down the other way. Any time you need the rascal, just drop by and I'll tell him to carry you there, Longarm."

Chapter 8

Longarm said he was much obliged and asked the livery man if he had horses for hire as well.

Thorp nodded, but said, "Not that you could ride to the den of the Grannywitch, now. You and my boy will have to walk where it's dry enough. May have to do some rafting as well. But my boy will get you there, one damn way or another."

Another man grunted, "I wouldn't go, even if the Grannywitch was younger and better-looking. She hates white men, and I don't care what they say that army man come down with, the Grannywitch *pizened* him. Some say she conjured up them springs from ground no springs had ever sprung from afore, as well!"

"Some has seen haunts out there by the big boils, too!" another townee warned. "I mind them Crawford folks as used to have a still a mile from the Grannywitch telling me they'd seen all sorts of dark shadowy spooks out yonder, about the time the flood fust came outten the Arkansas so mysterious."

Swanson snorted. "Oh, hell, the Grannywitch is just a fool old lunatic no others of her own kind will have anything to do with. The Crawford kids just made that up, likely after getting into their daddy's awful corn. Nobody else ever saw no haunts."

The other man insisted, "Sure they did. I heard other nesters tell of dark spooks flitting about through the trees out there late at night. They could tell they was spooks because, when you called out to 'em, they vanished, instead of answering like men would have. And don't you all remember how puzzled we was when that flood fust started?"

"I wasn't," Swanson said. "The damned river just come through the levee at flood time. It'd done it afore, you know."

"In high summer, at low water? How come them army men never found no break in the natural levee? One told me direct he thought the most water come up from them boils instead of the fool river! How do you account for that, Swanson?"

Swanson said, "It ain't my job to account for it. I'm a railroad man, not a hydraulics engineer. Mayhaps the boils come in from under the levee. Mayhaps they're a new spring from the Ozarks to the north. The notion the Grannywitch conjured 'em from hell is trash talk."

Longarm saw they were fixing to argue about it some and, since he doubted anyone here had a sensible explanation, he rose to leave, telling Thorp he'd drop by the livery in the morning. As he turned from the table he saw O'Carroll had already left. He'd figured all along the Irishman was sensible. Nobody argued when he left by the same front door. He walked back to the Western Union and had the night man send some wires for him. He brought Billy Vail up to date by night-letter rates, since there wasn't all that much to report, save for the killings he felt sure Billy would approve.

He went into the back room to get the list O'Carroll had told him of. He found the not-as-bright Mahoney holding the fort. Mahoney said O'Carroll had retired for the night with some town girl, but he gave Longarm the names of the missing local lawmen. Longarm took it back out front and put out an all-points requesting any suspicions anyone, anywhere, might have on names like Smith and Jones. He sent a few other checks on names he'd just learned and then, having done his duty for now, went back to the hotel to ask what might be the pleasure of Sylvia Norris of the Royal Society.

When she didn't answer his first discreet knock he decided she could be asleep and turned to go. But she opened her door and hauled him back in, saying, "Oh, I was afraid that Yankee bitch had her hooks in you again, darling."

He noticed the English girl's nails were digging into his back pretty good as she made him so welcome, hugging him tight against her open kimono. He kissed her, aiming to be polite. But when they came up for air he had to say, "Miss Tess and me never played hooky, Red. I just escorted her a spell for the Smithsonian and I ain't seen her since. You see, someone stole some field notes from her, and they suspicioned she might be in danger, so—"

"Never mind about her! What about me?" the redhead sobbed, reaching down to fumble with his fly buttons. It was a mighty interesting question. She could feel his dawning interest, too, as she fumbled in vain, not being used to the copper buttons Levi's had there mostly for serious riding, aboard a bigger critter.

He asked, "Are you in danger, too, Red?"

She laughed. "I'll know better in a minute. You seem to be somewhat taller than I assumed. Why don't we get

101

out of this ridiculous upright position and discuss it more comfortably?"

He didn't argue as she let go, moved to the bed, and shucked her kimono entire before climbing aboard the quilts. He made sure he kept track of his guns, of course, but he let everything else fall anywhere it had a mind to as he joined her on the bed. By the time he had, she was panting, "Hurry, hurry, can't you see I'm absolutely *gushing* for you!"

He couldn't see it, but he could sure feel it as he entered her. Sylvia raised her hips to meet his first thrust. She dug her nails into his bounding buttocks and hissed, "Oh, lovely! Try to make it last! I haven't had a man for months, and I'm burning with sheer lust tonight!"

He found that easy to believe.

As they lay cuddled and exhausted in the soft light, she crooned, "I was so afraid you'd just be another bunny rabbit. So many men are, you know, for all the brave talk."

He kissed her and sighed. "I wouldn't know. I hardly ever screw rabbits, boastful or no."

She chuckled and said, "I know. But you've obviously had lots of experience with *women*. Aren't you going to take it out now?"

"Do you want me to, Red?"

"Lord, no! Just let me get my breath back. I believe you, now, about that Smithsonian wench. You haven't had any in some time, either, have you?"

"I cannot tell a lie, I tore off some slap and tickle just a short spell ago. But you got prettier tits." He moved in her experimentally, and they went crazy some more for a spell.

Afterwards, she insisted on a breather. He lit a cheroot

to smoke while he let her breathe, her red hair unbound all over his naked chest as she snuggled her head in the hollow of his shoulder, telling him how great he was.

He asked, "You say Tess Winslow and them others is camped about here somewheres, Red? Funny, I ain't seen any of 'em since they carried her away."

"They're camped down the railway, on higher ground. Why do you ask? Surely you can't be interested in that icy slut at this late stage?"

He grimaced and said, "Icy and slut don't go together. A gal can be one or she can be the other. I don't know Tess well enough to have such opinions on her. How come *you* know so much about her, Red?"

"We're deadly rivals. Hadn't you guessed?"

"Well, that does sound true. What are you two pretty little things contesting so hard? I know to my chagrin it ain't me. Tess had her chance."

Sylvia laughed. "I didn't think she was as sporting as me when it came to gentlemen. I'm miffed at her, if you must know, because she came out with a paper on the western stage grouse a few months ago. *I* was the one who first noticed the territorial behavior of the species, you know!"

"I knew no such thing. How did she beat you to the punch? Do you *all* steal one another's field notes?"

"Not bloody likely. One can't be too careful with one's findings. A layman like you couldn't hope to know what a dot-eat-dog world the scientific community can be."

He said, "A spell back I met up with rival fossil hunters who were ready to kill one another over lizard bones. I'd have cracked the case a heap sooner had I known at first how serious you scientific folk take such things. I'm on another case entire, now. So I want you to listen tight before you fib to me, Red.

103

"I got me too many pieces of a puzzle the U.S. government is interested in. Getting some of the pieces out of the way would surely help. So I'd best warn you that, while petty theft and scaring folk ain't federal, lying to a federal officer is. You ain't a U. S. citizen. So, if you don't aim to go home sooner than you might have planned, you'd best cooperate with me, hear?"

"I'll do my best, darling. Would you like me to get on top?"

"We got plenty of time for that, after you fess up. Did you or did you not steal Miss Winslow's notes and fire a shot across her bows that time, just to discourage her some?"

"Oh, what an awful thing to accuse me of! What kind of a girl do you think I am, darling?"

"We've established that. You invited me in here just now to pump me as to what I might or might not know about the Smithsonian team. I'm willing to swap what I know for what you know, since it can't hurt anyone all that much. You go first. You was just out West, bird watching, too, if you know about sage hens. Fill in the rest for me. I promise I won't arrest you on petty charges if you can tell me whether Tess is in any real danger or not."

She sighed and said, "Well, maybe I did try to drive her away from some prairie I'd seen first. Her notes were of no use to me, in the end. She hadn't found out anything we don't all know about extinction versus survival of species. I hope you aren't angry with naughty little me, now?"

He hugged her tighter and said, "Honey, I've always admired naughty little gals, and you've no idea how good it feels to sweep that part of the puzzle off the table! I got another question. Tess says all of you are interested

104

in this stretch of drowned woodland because the pending shootoff might make things even worse. True or false?"

"True," she said. "I've already had some time to look about, and the biology here is in a dreadful state. It's changing as one looks at it. Just today I saw some orchard grass that must have sprouted under drier conditions, no more than a few weeks ago, so—"

"Yeah, yeah," he cut in, "everybody agrees that the water level's still rising. I'm going out in the morn for a look-see at them mysterious springs. Getting back to the shooting contest, that's starting in the morning, too, and Tess says the shooting figures to be terrible. Do you agree?"

"Of course. Given all the patches of new open water, some flocks are sure to drop in over the next ten days. But not many will *stay*. Waterfowl need food as well as water. Dry-rooted vegetation is all dead and sour. Water weeds haven't had time to establish themselves well enough to feed large flocks."

"I seen woodpeckers and robin sign this afternoon."

"Naturally. Woodpeckers thrive among dead trees, and robins are attracted to recently flooded farmlands. Worms, you know. There are all sorts of scattered opportunist feeders out there in that tangle at the moment. But serious shooting is another matter. Quail will be long gone. Ducks and geese won't stay long."

"Then how come you science folk are so interested, if you figure the big shootoff will be a bust?"

She snuggled closer and explained, "The contestants are hoping to see more birds than they probably will. We, as that snippy Tess told you, are as interested in what we *don't* see as what we may. The Tangleroost is an unusual freak of nature. It's an opportunity to see extinction and survival in the raw, without, for once, the hand of man involved. Or at least it would be, if those silly hunters weren't crowding in to complicate matters."

"Tess told me that, too. She said the Smithsonian's not in favor of such contests. What about you Royal folk?"

"Heavens, no nature-study group would be in favor of such a thing. Left to themselves, the migrating birds might strike some other natural balance. Some few might even adapt to the unusual conditions, as Professor Darwin suggests. But it's going to be bloody hard to decide whether a dead wood duck starved or ate fallen lead shot, now."

"I wouldn't want to be out there with a butterfly net while Calamity Jane and Sweet Sioux was shooting at anything that moved, neither. So tell me, do you think any serious bird lovers would do anything really serious to stop the big shootoff, Red?"

"Anything's possible, I suppose. But do you think someone's trying to stop the contest, dear?" she asked.

It was a good question. He said, "Not that I know of. The marshal who asked my help ain't here to tell me what in hell he expects to happen. But he must have had a reason to send out the call for help. Someone else must have had a reason to stop help from getting here. Far as I can tell, nobody's even made dirty faces at the *contestants* streaming in. I've yet to spy one wanted man in the crowd, and the only criminal activity I've uncovered has all been aimed at lawmen. I sure wish Moran would get back from Pine Bluff."

Sylvia began to fondle him as she said, "I've told you all I know. Now you want to tell me about those awful Smithsonian field workers, don't you?"

"I have," he said. "All I know, leastways. Your rivals see the situation the same way you do. I don't see what either of you would gain by keeping the law away as you count feathers."

"Oh, dear, does that mean you want to go?" she began. Then, as she started stroking harder, she laughed and added, "I see you'd rather *come* some more." So they did. It wasn't as if he had anyplace better to go, *or* come, that night.

Chapter 9

Next morning, at the livery stable, Longarm found the thirteen-year-old Calvin Thorp raring to go. Young Calvin was light-skinned, but it was just as likely the Thorps had owned his folk before the War. Arkansas had been mostly Confederate. It would have been rude to ask, at this late date, how young Calvin had come by his last name.

The boy lit out ahead of him barefoot. He paid little heed to puddles, and Longarm's army boots were soon soaked through as they wound ever deeper into the Tangleroost. From time to time a shotgun blasted in the distance and Calvin laughed as he said fool strangers were already out hunting ducks where no ducks, in Calvin's opinion, were likely to be found. Longarm didn't ask the colored boy what he thought they were shooting at instead. He knew some old boys just couldn't take a gun into the woods without shooting something. It sure played hell with windmill blades, signposts, and such.

Calvin led him around a small, sluggish lake with a stone chimney rising from the scummy water and pointed it out as the old Peterson homestead. A crane was perched atop the chimney, morosely staring down at the scum. Nobody had shot it yet, but if it didn't spy a frog soon, it figured to fly on.

Longarm kept an eye on the sky as Calvin led him in what sure felt like circles. The sun said he could trust the boy after all. They were cutting around a mess of jackstrawed fallen trees and what Calvin called man-eating ground, but Longarm saw they were trending in general toward the Arkansas.

Later they heard shots ahead of them and the boy stopped, saying, "That's funny, Mistah Longarm. They ain't supposed to be nobody huntin' over that way. It'd be off the contest grounds."

"Mayhaps someone's cheating. The hunting has to be better over near the river, where things is more natural. How far are we from the Grannywitch now?"

The boy pointed more or less ahead. "Less'n a mile. Uh, does you mind if I wait out in the trees while you jaw with the conjure woman, Mistah Longarm?"

"I don't mind. But how come? Are you scared of her, Calvin?"

"Yessuh. All us colored folk is. She got the Power!"

"So I hear tell. But would she use 'em against her own kind?"

"She ain't my kind, Mistah Longarm. They says the Grannywitch is *Injun*. Injun and white, leastways. My daddy say in the old days some Injuns would take colored folk in and others would scalp you. So it's best not to mess with any Injuns, and the Grannywitch is a *witch!*"

Longarm wasn't in the mood to argue the point. He knew white folk who wore shoes had murdered poor old women in Salem Town at one time for acting a mite odd or just being unpopular with their neighbors. He wasn't worried about the Grannywitch turning him into a frog, but he sure hoped she wouldn't shoot him. Eccentrics living alone could be sort of spooky whether they were in direct contact with the devil or not.

The Grannywitch didn't shoot Longarm. He left Calvin at the treeline and circled out across an open field where a wide pond bubbled in the sunlight before overflowing into the lower swamp beyond. Like the spring, the gray shack of the mysterious Grannywitch was on unusually high ground for the Tangleroost. He waved his Winchester polite and called out to the cabin as he approached. There was no answer. As he got closer, he heard flies—lots of flies; bluebottles—and moved in faster.

It was hard to tell if the woman sprawled face up on the dirt floor just inside her open door had been spooky or whatever, with her dead face masked by all those carrion flies. The smell wasn't too bad yet, so he allowed she'd died, or been killed, within the last twenty-four hours.

He didn't want to, but he had to kneel by her side to brush the flies away with his hat. He could see, then, that she'd been a fairly handsome breed of about fifty. The bullethole was in her forehead.

He stood up, found a quilt on a rustic bedstead, and covered the corpse. He hastily examined the rest of the interior for clues. He found no shell casings or signed confessions. There was a stack of old newspapers in the corner, indicating the woman had been able to read. She had crude shelves stacked with jars of herbs including, sure enough, some dried leaves that smelled a lot like the cheroots Tess wouldn't let him smoke. But he imagined any spey woman worth her salt would have some henbane handy. In moderation, it gave one mighty powerful dreams.

He'd about finished when he noticed that a plant growing in a coffee can on one windowsill looked sick. He wondered why a woman of any kind would plant a flower and then not water it. So he gave the plant a yank and, sure enough, there was an oilcloth packet under the dry dirt in the can. He opened it and whistled, wondering how a spey woman living alone in a swamp had come by over a hundred in Union, not Confederate, bills. He put the money in a pocket of his denim jacket and put the plant back in the can to die some more. Then he went to have a look at the mysterious boil in the Grannywitch's front yard.

As he stared soberly down at the big spring he said, "No offense, Lord, but it's true You do move in mysterious ways. I know places further West where this much water could cause a range war, and the folk around here already had more water than they ever wanted."

The boil was about forty feet across, coming up in a way to rival some tourist attractions in Yellowstone. He dropped to one knee, put a finger in, and had a taste. He grimaced and spat. It was sour as vinegar. He said, "Wherever you come from, you ain't water from the Arkansas. River water's bad enough, but you're just awful!"

He moved around to where it overflowed, running the tip of his tongue against his teeth as he decided it had to be sulfur acid in the water. It was small wonder the Tangleroost was so dead, and the sassy Halifax sisters had told him there were other boils around here.

He found them, in time, with no help from Calvin. When he rejoined the boy and told him the witch was

111

dead, Calvin took off running and never looked back.

But Longarm knew where he was now, so he just poked on south of the dead woman's place and, sure enough, found another acid-water boil less than a hundred yards away, this one in a tangle of long-dead blackberry brush. He found a third welling up through a tangle of fallen timber. He could tell the trees had been there minding their own leafy business when all hell had come up through their roots and killed them. He didn't look for more. The boils he'd found, alone, were enough to account for the slowly rising level of the whole swamp. Not being an army engineer, he didn't know what to do about them, either. So he headed back to town.

The experience recalled to mind a raw spring morn a much younger Custis Long had been advancing through some other woods as point man on a dismounted recon patrol. There was the same lonely silence in his vicinity and the same constant crackle of gunfire in the mysterious distance. Most of it seemed to be coming from the railroad causeway ahead. He looked up and failed to see why. High in the blue above the dead treetops a V of tiny dots was winging north. The geese were hopelessly out of range, and had they ever been interested in the Tangleroost to begin with, all that wild gunfire surely would have discouraged them from flying down.

Longarm shrugged and moved on. A short time later he had the clear opportunity for a wing shot at a sparrow bird, but he passed on it. He didn't shoot a redwing sassing him from a dead branch, either. It was sort of interesting that both birds he did see in the flood-killed forest were the kinds one spied around the haunts of man. He was beginning to grasp what the two bird-watching gals had said about upsetting the balance of nature. While some shy critters seemed to dry up and blow away the first summer the sod got busted, others, if anything, increased. He knew there were jackrabbits hopping about the vacant lots of Denver, while buffalo were said to be might scarce inside the city limits. If the rising water hadn't been so sour, by now there would at least have been some decent fishing and frogging, mayhaps muskrat trapping, to replace the lost resources of the Tangleroost. But nothing most folk had any use for thrived on sulfur water. The dark, slimy ponds all about reminded him of the drainage ditches and settling ponds of a mining town. Trash fish like suckers and pup-carp might manage. But the extinction the science folk were so interested in was spreading wider by the day around here, and he was damned if he found it interesting. It was just depressing, and he still had no notion what Moran had wanted with extra help.

He spied a familiar cabin beside a wider lake ahead and wisely swung well wide of it. He wasn't mad at the Halifax sisters, but a man had to save his strength, and the sweet little fools hadn't been able to tell him anything about the Tangleroost that wasn't common knowledge. His detour led him through a sickly cane brake, the reeds just holding their own in the unwholesome water, to where an abandoned country cemetery lay half flooded with some markers rising from still-dry mounds and others standing ankle-deep in fetid floodwater. Here and there a dying stalk of this year's green-up showed how the graveyard had just been flooded in the past few days. He straightened a tilted cross with his free hand and marveled aloud, "I wonder how long this is supposed to go on. Seems to me a ditch through the levee would have to drain off at least *some* of this shit. For the river can't be near as high right now."

He moved on, looking for the wagon trace that had

113

to run from the graveyard back to town. He found it, followed it a quarter of a mile, then cursed when he saw it dipped under an open sheet of fairly shallow but mighty wide water. His feet were already wet, of course. But now that he knew how acid the water was, he didn't want to ruin the leather of his boots more than he had to. Even it if was less acid than vinegar it couldn't be doing his socks much good, and he knew he'd best wash his feet with lye soap before he pulled on a fresh pair from his possibles.

He saw he could work around to his left, so that was the way he went. He was busting through some still-surviving blackberry canes when, above the crackle of gunfire ahead, he heard a woman yelling fit to bust. So he bulled on through the stickerbrush to see why.

As he burst out the far side he spied a tumbledown abandoned cabin, or one that should have been. But blue smoke rose from the stovepipe sticking through the shingles and, in the doorway, Tess Winslow, of all gals, was struggling with two rough, raggedy gents who looked as if they hadn't shaved *or* had a woman for some time.

Each had Tess by one arm, so she couldn't get at the gun under her button-down skirt. The skirt was open above one knee, reading two ways. They'd either grabbed her before she could get at her garter holster, or the skirt had come undone in the fight. Longarm didn't ask. Not wanting to hit the wrong target in that three-way tussle, he sent a .44-40 into the muck at his side and levered another round in the chamber of his Winchester as he called out, "Morning, you all. Is this a private party, or can any number join?"

It was not true that a barefoot, frightened colored boy could run as fast as two grown white men in soggy boots. As they lit out like scalded cats in opposite directions,

Tess, left in the lurch, wound up on her ass in the doorway. Longarm let the rascals go, for now. He walked over to help the girl up, asking soberly, "I'd sure like to know whether I just saved your virtue or ruined your whole morning, ma'am."

She wrapped herself around him, sobbing, "Oh, thank God you got here in time! I think they meant to . . . You know!"

"I figured as much. Before you tell me who they was, tell me what in thunder possessed you to come clean out here unescorted! In fairness to all concerned, a she-male wandering about pure helpless is considered fair game by some of our gamier backwoodsmen."

"They were in the cabin," she said. "I didn't know anyone was still living here. I meant to use it as a bird blind, see?"

He unwrapped himself from her as he growled, "I'm starting to see, Goldilocks. Stand clear while I make sure there was only two bears, this time."

He slipped into the one-room cabin, crabbing to one side just in case, but saw it was just a stinky den where two dirty men had been staying a spell. Bedrolls were spread on the dirt floor. Either one would have served as well to spread old Tess on, and she would have found either just as sweat-grimed. A pot of beans was simmering on the corner stove. Longarm put them aside lest they burn. Tess came in, wrinkling her nose as she opined how awful it smelled in here.

He nodded but said, "They must have been more pleasantly surprised. I'm glad I didn't have to gun either one. It was your fault, no offense."

She gasped. "Custis! How could you think I'm that kind of girl?"

He sighed. "I know you ain't. But you was still out

of line. How was *they* to know what kind of gal you was? Shy virgins hardly ever approach a lonesome cabin sprouting smoke. They must have knowed about all them new fancy gals at the saloon. So they put your fancy duds together with your approach, and you know the rest."

"Damn it, Custis, I distinctly told them I was no such thing!"

"I know. I heard you nigh a quarter mile off. But as a gal in Denver and me were discussing a few days ago, some men tend to assume a gal is just funning when she says no."

"Oh, you're just horrid!" she sobbed, turning for the door.

Longarm snapped, "Don't. I mean it. It ain't safe for you to run loose in the Tangleroost without a leash, and I ain't through here."

She stopped in the doorway, but stood there tapping her foot as he rumaged through the possibilities of the men he'd scared off. She asked him what on earth he was looking for and he said, "Don't know. Ain't found it yet. I can't help wondering what them jaspers might have been doing out here, aside from laying in wait for you, that is. There's plenty of nicer abandoned buildings closer to the tracks. They wasn't hunting more serious game than you or I'd see some serious guns and shotgun shells around here someplace. All they had was their sidearms which, lucky for all of us, they never thought to draw before they ran off."

He found a well-thumbed book with a plain brown paper cover. He opened it, decided Tess was too young to look at such pictures, and pocketed it to read later. A man just couldn't know too many positions when he met

116

up with a natural athlete. "We'd best get back to town," he said.

She said, "It's still early. I came out here to take field notes, and I'd barely started when those awful men . . ."

"We're going back, anyways. I have to, because I have a death to report to the coroner. You have to because I say so. Where's your notebook?"

She patted a breast pocket of her whipcord habit. "I don't know what happened to my pencil, damn it."

"It's likely trampled in the mud forever. Come on. I'll tell you all about the muck and mire out here as we get the hell out of it. Let me go first, and you stay tight as a tick behind me. Them gents could be sore losers, and there's a whole mess of other lunatics with guns up ahead."

As they gingerly made their way through the swamp, he brought her up to date on the Grannywitch and her mysterious boils. When he mentioned the acid water, she wanted to go back and get samples. He snorted in disgust. "The whole damn swamp is filled with the same, girl. The water's coming from them boils, not the Arkansas."

He thought that had settled the matter for now. But as they passed a scummy pond, Tess made him stop while she got out a bitty leather-cased kit. She hunkered down gingerly and filled a small glass vial. Then she took out a sheet of litmus paper, tore off a slip, and dunked it in the pond. The paper turned pink. She said he was right about it being acidic and he said he'd already told her that, adding, "Once you've been around old mines you know the smell. I tasted it, besides."

She sniffed the damp litmus. "I'll have to test our sample back in camp to be certain, but it does smell more like sulfuric acid than the humic acid we'd assumed.

How do you imagine that could be, Custis?"

He held out a hand to help her up again. "Don't know," he said. "What in tarnation is humic acid?"

As she moved on with him she explained that humic acid was natural in most sour soils. It was made by bugs out of rotting vegetation and the air. She said there was no call for so much sulfur in the water.

He shrugged. "I've seen sulfur springs in lots of places. I read somewhere it comes from deep in the bedrock. So there goes the notion of capping them boils. Old Nick must have busted through down below to drain his hellish bathtubs."

"There *are* hot sulfur springs in Arkansas, but this area isn't supposed to be volcanic. How hot would you say those new springs were, Custis?"

He frowned and replied, "They ain't hot at all. They'd be sort of cold to swim in, this time of the year, if a man wanted to dip his hide in vinegar. What gave you the notion I said they was hot sulfur springs, Tess?"

"I just assumed they were, Custis. I've never heard of *cold* sulfur springs, have you?"

He didn't answer until they'd moved on a spell. Then he said, "I got to find me a book on geology. Is there any natural law saying sulfur water can't cool as it wanders about down under? Like I said, old mines ooze stinkwater all the time, and it ain't hot."

They went on, with her jawing on and on about the mysterious enough springs in the big-worded way of her mysterious trade. He was more interested in keeping them from getting shot for geese than he was about even his own wet socks. So when he heard another woman's voice cry out, "Oh, I sees something, Sweet Sioux!" he

118

called out, "Hold your fire, you infernal buffalo skinners! It's me, and they don't give prizes on my species, even here!"

Calamity Jane called back, "Is that my true love, Longarm?" Even Sweet Sioux had to laugh at that notion. Longarm looked more disgusted than amused as he and Tess joined Calamity Jane and the even uglier Sweet Sioux in a clearing near the tracks. As Tess gingerly shook hands with old Calamity, the boisterous Queen of Deadwood, as she now called herself, said, "I might have knowed he was sparking another gal in the woods. But that's all right, honey. He's man enough for both of us. Why don't we all go back to my camp, bust out the likker, and have us a real orgy? The shooting out here ain't good for shit this morning!"

Tess gulped, turned pink as her litmus paper had, and said she'd heard of the famous Calamity Jane. Sweet Sioux asked, wistfully, if she'd read what Ned Buntline had writ about *him* in his Wild West penny dreadful. Tess gallantly lied she had, so the battered old hide-skinner grinned down at her like a lovesick kid and said, "Calamity's just funning, Missy. Like old Ned writ, us natural nobility of the frontier ever acts like gents around ladies, hear?"

Calamity Jane told him to speak for himself. Longarm cut her off and said, "We just brushed with a couple of rustic gents who didn't seem so noble. Did you see two bearded rascals pass this way, sudden? One had on a blue shirt and the other wore what might have been red and black checks when it was cleaner."

Calamity Jane asked if they were good-looking. Longarm said, "Never mind. It was dumb to ask *you* if

119

you'd seen two strangers in pants, Calamity. Can we get to the tracks from here without getting shot, do you reckon?"

Sweet Sioux pointed with his shotgun muzzle. "Cinder path, just t'other side of that fallen elm. There's other shooting from the tracks, but mostly *up*. Don't reckon they'll take you two for deer once you're in the open."

"I hope not. How come you two forged this deep in the tangle?"

Sweet Sioux shrugged. "Ain't nothing dumb enough to fly along the tracks. We hoped to spy some setting ducks in the woods. See any, Longarm?"

"Yesterday, in modest numbers. Squatter gals got 'em all with a punt gun. Ain't nothing out there right now but sparrows and blackbirds."

Calamity Jane said, "Hot damn. Let's go git 'em, Sweet Sioux!"

The big breed looked dubious. "I feels sure the contest judges had something more like ducks and geese in mind, Calamity."

But she asked, "Where did it say that in the contest rules? It just said the hunter as bags the most *birds* in one day gits the prize for that day, right?"

"Sure, but . . . sparrow birds?"

"A bird's a bird, ain't it? Look on the bright side, Sweet Sioux. A hundred bitty birds is easier to tote home than one fat whooping crane or Canada as only counts for one kill!"

The two of them wandered on into the Tangleroost, still debating the point. Longarm chuckled and took the Smithsonian gal's arm to head her the other way over fallen timber. Tess grimaced and said, "I don't find those two disgusting vagrants at all amusing."

120

"Neither do I," he said. "I remember them both as younger and prettier. I was laughing at Calamity's fool notion. When you study on it, it makes sense. Wouldn't it be funny if the winner of this first day's contest copped the prize with one extra bluejay?"

"Oh, my God, no wonder she calls you her true love! Don't you have any respect for nature at all?"

He shrugged. "Sure. You'd be surprised how natural I feel at times. I ain't here to shoot our feathered friends, Miss Tess. If it was up to me, I'd call the disgusting business off. But I'm here to enforce the law, not to balance nature."

He didn't see why that should make her so mad, but it must have. For as soon as he had her safely back in town, she lit off on him again without even saying thanks.

Chapter 10

O'Carroll was commanding the day watch at the telegraph office again. Longarm thought at first he was looking so pleased with himself because of the local gal he was sparking. But the young Irishman said, "You just missed all the fun, Longarm. I just sent Doyle and Fagin up the line with our prisoners."

"We got prisoners?"

"We do. This is to say, we just arrested them as they came tearing into town from the woods, woild-eyed. Doyle and Fagin naturally wanted a word with thim because of the odd way they was after running and looking back over their shoulders as they passed our back door. One was after slapping leather on Doyle, and so now he don't even *walk* fast, though the doctor said it wasn't a serious wound at all, at all. When the boyos hauled thim in here for doctoring and questioning it was meself made the grand connection between their fuzzy faces and the shaven versions of some old faded fliers. The one Doyle shot in the thigh was wanted for army desertion as well as armed robbery. The other was only wanted for robbery, which is why he didn't feel as much of a need for bravery, I'd be after thinking. As we was all waiting for the train to Pine Bluff I persuaded the more timid one to tell me the whole story. They'de been hoiding in an abandoned shack in the swamp all this time. They said some other outlaw jumped their claim and drove them off with a Winchester."

Longarm chuckled and said that sounded logical enough. Then he asked O'Carroll what their names might have been. The Irishman laughed and said, "Faith, that's the part that's rich. On the Wanted fliers, they was Waterman and Seares. But until the great shootoff attracted so much public attention to this tiny town they went by Smith and Jones, and you'll never guess the jobs they was holding so bold and bare-faced."

"Town law?"

"Aw, Jasus, ye guessed. I had a serious discussion with Mayor Swanson about the matter just now, when we put the prisoners on one of his darling trains. Swanson said he'd had no idea they was wanted criminals. He said they told him they was retired railroad dicks."

Longarm shrugged. "It might work. Few railroad section bosses are likely to keep old Wanted fliers among their dispatches. I have to talk to him myself, so I'll double-check his tale."

O'Carroll scowled and said, "Hold on, now, Longarm. It was the Pine Bluff office made the collar, not Denver, damn it!"

"Now don't get your bowels in an uproar, old son. I ain't out to steal no credit from you boys. I have to tell Swanson in his capacity as coroner that there's a dead woman stinking up the Tangleroost, too."

"That's different. Dead woman, you say? Do you think thim two we just arrested could have done it?"

123

"Don't know. Somebody did. But, as long as we're being so damned picky, it was the Colorado office as found the the body. So don't worry your pretty little head about it."

He turned to go. O'Carroll tagged along, saying, "Jasus, can't ye take a joke, Longarm? We'd be glad to share the credit with yez if the two cases tie together!"

"I'm sure you would, Sean. It was my fool notion from the first that we was all working for the same Justice Department. So what's it going to be? Do you want to work with me as a professional lawman or are we having a contest, too, like them fool duck-shooters?"

O'Carroll must have wanted in on the murder of the Grannywitch, for he stuck close as a tick while Longarm went to look for Swanson. He explained grudgingly, "I was thrained to work as part of a team myself, you know. But it's not easy working under that damned auld Moran. You see, he's given to stealing credit, and . . . well, it's more ambitious than that I am."

"I never would have guessed. What do you mean about Moran taking credit? A head marshal's *supposed* to get the credit for what his team does. My boss does so all the time."

"That may be true, Longarm. But does your name appear at all, at all on the papers forwarded to Washington?"

"Well, sure. The Washington office expects full reports, in infernal triplicate, and nobody expects even Billy Vail to make arrests, personal, sitting in his swivel chair."

O'Carroll sighed. "I knew I was working for the wrong federal district. A few weeks ago I made a grand collar, all by meself, when I recognized a wanted queer passer in me very own bank as I was cashing me paycheck. He put up a fight and pinked me with his derringer before I had him on the floor with the cuffs on. I felt sure, as I hauled him kicking and screaming the length of Pine Bluff, that I'd at least get a pat on me head in the dispatches. But, according to Moran, he did it all himself, including the shoot-out in the bank! Does that sound fair?"

Longarm smiled crookedly and replied, "No. It sounds like an army outfit I served in one time. Our C.O. was baby-shit yellow, and nobody could ever figure out where he was when the enemy was within ten miles. But he still wound up with more medals than the rest of us. You can't buck the system, Irish. The big shots always hog the credit. But look at it from their point of view. When they was still *little* shots, *they* got robbed of a lot of credit. So it tends to even out. I don't worry about such things no more. As long as I know what I done, and I didn't get killed doing it, I figure I'm ahead."

By this time they had reached the railroad dispatch shack by the water tower. Sure enough, the mayor, coroner, and likely part-time saloon swamper was on duty behind his rolltop desk. Longarm told him what he had found at the shack of the Grannywitch. Swanson sighed, said he was on more serious duty at the moment and that the dead nigger gal would likely keep until he got off duty.

Longarm said, "She wasn't colored. She was mayhaps half Natchez, like the real colored folk around here said. Just when do you get off duty, Coroner?"

"Soon as the next train comes in, around four-thirty. It's a special, bringing a mess of hunters for the contest. That's why I have to stay here myself instead of letting one of my helpers man this damned desk. The railroad raises hell if a switchman or water jerk's on duty when a train jumps the tracks and, as soggy as the siding's got of late—"

Longarm cut in to say he understood that problem. Then he asked, "How come you can't pump water away from the yards, at least? You got a pump for that water tower, right?"

"Sure. Have to. The water has to run from higher than the engine when she stops for water. We used to pump harder. Now the well water's a lot less deep. As to pumping water away from the tracks, where the hell *to?* Can't you see the water's riz some, lately?"

"I've noticed that. It's higher on the side away from the river, too. A good six or eight feet. Ain't it that side that's doing the most to threaten your embankment?"

Swanson frowned up at him. "Are you a civil engineer, too?"

Longarm replied, "Nope. I just got common sense. If you had so much as one culvert under the causeway, the water pressure on both sides of the track would soon be the same, you know."

Swanson sighed and said, "I didn't think you'd ever worked for a railroad. I got common sense, too. I've *asked* authorization to drain *more* than the high water on the north side of the tracks. Any fool can see that it would only take a week or so to punch a ditch through the higher ground to the south and drain half the flooded land overnight."

"And the railroad said no? How come?"

Swanson shrugged. "The head office says I have no call putting railroad employees to work on a land reclamation project unless the railroad owns the land. Some dude engineer who's really more a lawyer says we could get sued for damages if a mess of fallen timber and acid

126

water was suddenly to go down the main channel of the Arkansas, unannounced."

"What about your soggy situation right here? Couldn't you at least let the water pressure to the north drain away?"

"Sure I could. It wouldn't take but a few days to dig the culvert. But I keep getting the same answer. They say anything I do to upset the water levels hereabouts can do some damage to some damned body, and that they'd rather leave nature to take her own course. You can't sue even a railroad over natural disasters."

O'Carroll, who had been listening from the doorway, yawned and said he'd best get back to his own post. For an ambitious young lawman, he didn't fancy detail much. Longarm stayed put to ask the railroader, "How do your duties as section boss square with your duty to the community you're mayor and such of? Couldn't you, as mayor, order the levee breached as a township operation?"

Swanson said, "Not hardly. For one thing, the town don't have the manpower. For another, me and everyone with a shovel would likely get fired on the spot when the railroad found out about it. Almost all the able-bodied men I could use are, like myself, on the payroll of the railroad. And they've ordered me, direct, not to mess with the forces of nature. I'm only six years short of a gold watch and a pension. I don't owe the township an old age spent in poverty."

Longarm frowned. "No offense, but that sounds like a modest insult to my intelligence. Just last night you told me you and your partners had control of the local land company, Swanson. And I couldn't help noticing, as I just passed the saloon, that it was open full blast.

127

You and your pards own *that*, too, right?"

Swanson sighed and said, "It's a good thing I've mellowed some in my old age. There was a time I'd have taken you to fist city for calling me a liar. It's true that this dumb contest might allow our land holding company to almost break even. The extra rent we'll reap in the next ten days may pay us back the cash we laid out to buy up the titles of abandoned homesteads. Then what? When that contest ends, the whores as well as the hunters will be gone, and we'll have a rising swamp all to ourselves to get rich on."

"What if you drained the swamp? Seems to me you and a handful of other charitable gents would have a whole township, six by six miles of bottomland, for lease or sale."

Swanson swore softly. "There you go again, damn it! I just told you, I'm not about to quit or get fired just to drain a swamp with my own sweat and money. Before you point out that I stand to make a killing if I did, talk to the Army Corps of Engineers. Jesus Christ, didn't you think we *knew* what we'd have when we snapped up all those useless titles cheap?"

"Cheap title to expensive bottomland, if it was reclaimed."

"You left out the big if. Those army men saw things the same way, until they tested the unwanted spring water, too late. The Tangleroost hasn't just been flooded. It's been poisoned. Sure, a very expensive drainage ditch from the acid boils to the river would stop the water from rising. Then everyone downstream for miles would sue to stop that shit from getting into the Arkansas. Let's say we won. Anything's possible. Then what? Those army men told us that even if we installed all sorts of floodgates and drained the whole swamp, it would still take years,

128

maybe thirty or more, to restore the ruined soil to the way it was to begin with. We'd have to let it flood every year with clean rainwater, then open the sluices to drain it and dry it some more. I ain't got thirty years to wait. Not when the government's giving land away *free*, out on the high plains!"

Longarm nodded, but said, "I've seen some of the homesteads left out West, lately. It's more alkali than acid. Good land is going to have to be *bought* off someone from here on. The free cream's been skimmed."

"You want to buy a couple of sections of the Tangleroost? I can get you the whole swamp cheap, and, in ten days, my partners would be glad to throw in the leasehold under the saloon or, hell, the whole business block. You'd be surprised how business is around here most of the time."

Longarm said he wouldn't and that it was more like nine and a half days, now. He left the dispatch office and wandered over to the hotel to see how the contest was going.

It wasn't going at all, despite all the gunsmoke above the dead trees out back. Slade, the front man for the ammo company, was just having breakfast in the hotel dining room, alone. Longarm sat down across from him, ordered steak and eggs, and asked how come. Slade said, "We don't have to judge anything before sundown. Me and the panel will tally the day's bag in the saloon next door. Hey, would you like to be a judge?"

"Not hardly. I might drop by to see who won. At the rate things are going, you may wind up paying a thousand dollars for four-and-twenty blackbirds, not even baked in a pie. I wouldn't bet on a full four-and-twenty, neither!"

He told the puzzled Slade what Calamity Jane had

said about a bird being a bird. Slade looked upset. "I'm not sure they want me to count bitty songbirds, for God's sake!"

"Well, for your sake, you'd best have a better argument than that for Calamity and Sweet Sioux. She's really good with a bullwhip, and Sweet Sioux can act even meaner when he feels folk are taking advantage of him. Why not talk it over with them other judges? Did you say some of 'em was local big shots?"

Slade nodded and said that Parson Moore and the livery man, Thorp, had agreed to help out. The other judges he named were due on the afternoon train. Longarm didn't write them down. He got to work on his steak and eggs. But Slade was one of them city dudes who liked to talk while he ate. He kept pestering Longarm about the big shootoff that was supposed to be going on at the moment, and was, judging by the constant rumble of gunfire out back.

Longarm washed some steak down with coffee and said, "In ten days, who's to say? We're on a natural flyway, dismal as this part of it may be. You'll likely see a few good flocks before it's over. If fool passengers recall this flooded woodland fondly, you'll be up all night counting dead birds. Passengers got no sense at all. They just roost anywhere, when they get tired of flying."

Slade grimaced. "Well, at least a pigeon is a game bird. How were we to know we'd picked the one spot in the whole damned valley that we shouldn't have?"

"I sent a wire behind your back about that, Slade. I'm glad to report you don't seem to be up to anything worse than poor judgement. It really was your bosses, and not you, who chose this flooded bottomland. The name Tangleroost must have confused 'em. I reckon once, a

130

mess of birds roosted in that tangle out back. Now that I know how pure of heart you might be, I got me another question. You say your company leased the Tangleroost as a shooting ground. How much did it cost you?"

"Longarm, I'm not sure that's any business of yours."

"Sure it is. I just made it my business. Your turn."

Slade hesitated, then shrugged and said, "Oh, hell, you could get it from the front office with a court order and, knowing you, you would. We leased the woods for a thousand dollars."

"The whole swamp? The whole ten days?"

"Sure. What else is it good for now? Frankly, I think we were cheated."

Longarm nodded in agreement, and chewed the numbers along with more steak. "That don't add up to a motive for much, since there's at least a dozen partners in the land-holding company, giving each less than a hundred to murder over. Would you have paid more, had they insisted?" he asked.

"I guess so. I didn't get much argument about the price. The title holders seem to be more divided on whether they wanted the contest at all than they were about the price. Some fought like hell to keep us from holding the hunt at all. But most found it a harmless way to pick up some pocket money. So they voted our way in the end."

"Do you recall just who voted yes or no, Slade?"

"I wasn't there. They voted on it in secret, or at least at a meeting I was never invited to."

Longarm started to ask a dumb question. Then he realized a man who didn't attend a land-holders' meeting would hardly know who kept the minutes of said meetings. So he dug into his apple pie and by the time he'd put away a second slice Slade had finished and gone off somewhere to worry about Calamity Jane's awful notion.

Longarm enjoyed an after-dessert cheroot with more black coffee as he studied his next moves. He was running out of them. As he'd told Billy Vail from the start, there didn't really seem to be a pressing need here for the services of five local deputies and a mess of outside help. He finally got up, went back to the Western Union, and wired Denver the same. He sent the wire day rates so Vail would know he meant it when he said he wanted to come home. It was too bad about the murdered spey woman and about the once-green bottomland, but he'd seen nothing, so far, calling for so many lawmen.

Then, after he'd sent the wire, he got to wondering again why someone had gone to so much trouble to keep him from looking at all the nothing-much around here. So he went to look some more.

Chapter 11

Nobody had potted four-and-twenty anything by sundown. The day's shootoff was won by a farm boy from
Iowa who brought in a sick goose, half a dozen mallards,
and a great horned owl. The judges told Calamity Jane
the stray chicken she tried to add to her string of six
songbirds was just silly.

Longarm was surprised when Jacob Slade wrote out
a thousand-dollar check for the young Iowan. He took
the kid aside and advised him not to cash it until he got
home. The farm boy allowed he'd already figured that
out and was leaving on the next train north. He said he'd
never seen such piss-poor hunting in any woods, or such
hungry whores in any saloon, so he aimed to quit while
he was ahead. Some of the other discouraged hunters
had already announced the contest was a waste of time,
if not a downright fraud. But they mellowed some when
Slade told the barkeeps to serve consolation to all the
contestants.

Longarm didn't think he rated a free drink, and he
had to consider where he meant to spend the night, since
Vail hadn't answered his last wire one way or the other.

He and Sylvia had parted sort of friendly that morning, and he hadn't had any better offers, so he headed next door to see if she was still fond of him. He hadn't seen any of the professional bird watchers at the tally in the saloon.

He went out and headed for the hotel next door. Then a male voice hissed him into the narrow gap between the buildings. Longarm put his gun back in its holster when the other gent flashed a federal badge in the gloom and identified himself as Marshal Moran in the mysterious flesh. As the older man led him out back of the hotel he explained, "Nobody knows I came back on the four-thirty special. I recognized you from Billy Vail's description and that Colorado crush to your Stetson. We got some serious stuff to discuss in private."

They sat down on the back-door steps of the hotel kitchen and lit up. Moran asked what Longarm thought of his deputies so far. Longarm shook out his match and replied, "Tolerable. A mite green, but I reckon they mean well. Why ask me? Wasn't you the one who hired 'em?"

Moran sighed. "Yes and no. You might have guessed my name wasn't Mexican. But my folk come to Texas back in Forty-eight."

"I notice you talk more Texas than O'Carroll, no offense. Did you hire him, or didn't you?"

"I was pressured into it by District Judge O'Hara. And if you think O'Carroll talks with a brogue, wait until you hear O'Hara. They've Irished up on me, Longarm. I'm American as you and Billy Vail, so I just don't know what they're talking about when they mutter together in the Gaelic and sort of snicker at my orders."

Longarm blew a thoughtful smoke ring and mused aloud, "Seems to me if I was in command I'd just tell 'em to shape up or transfer out."

Moran said, "It ain't that simple. You see, I just found out both Judge O'Hara and the crew he pressured me into hiring for the Justice Department are paid-up members of the Fenian Society. You know about them, of course?"

Longarm nodded. "Sure. They been writing nasty letters to Queen Victoria and then pissing in her mailboxes for years. A mess of 'em raided Canada right after the War. They're supposed to be a secret society dedicated to freeing Ireland, only they talk about it so much it's hardly a secret."

Moran scowled darkly. "Some of the ringleaders are more dangerous. I've reason to suspect O'Hara's one of the inner circle."

Longarm frowned thoughtfully. "Well, I don't know what our own State Department has to say about home rule for Ireland. A lot of congressmen owe their seats to Irish ward bosses. But if you suspicion Judge O'Hara of acting against the interests of these United States, I reckon you ought to report it to somebody higher up the totem pole than me."

"How? Can't you see they got me boxed in, Longarm? Every move I make is reported to the district judge above me, likely in the Gaelic. Damn it, son, they just poisoned my kid, as a not-so-gentle warning!"

Longarm said, "I was the one as sent you the word about henbane as the likely cause of his ague. How is he, by the way?"

"Recovered totally, thanks to you, and the doc knowing what to do, once he knowed what it was. That's how I know I can trust you. You got to help me, Longarm."

"Do what, for God's sake? You sent out a call saying you had a big case here. Are you saying now it was office politics instead of at least a post-office robbery?"

"Can't you see how serious the Fenians are? They tried to poison you and the other help I sent away for. You were the only one who got through. It's a nation-wide plot, I tell you!"

Longarm smoked and thought some before he said, "It is sort of odd, someone tried to drug federal agents far and wide. But whey the hell would an Irish secret society want to do a thing like that?"

"To take over the government, of course! You just said yourself, the Irish control politics in lots of towns of late. O'Hara's a federal judge with the powers of life and death over my district! Having failed to take Ireland back from the English, the Fenians are out to take *our* country away from *us!*"

Longarm shook his head. "Sorry. That just won't wash. Ireland ain't no bigger than a single Southern state, and we both know how the Confederacy made out. How the hell could an outfit as can't take one bitty island away from England hope to take the U. S. away from the rest of us? The Germans and Chinese wouldn't like that at all."

"If you're so smart, who slipped you them henbane cigars?" Moran insisted.

"They was cheroots. I'm still working on that. I never said *everyone* in this country was pure of heart. I just can't it as their work. I know Sean O'Carroll's sort of pushy. I've had to push him back a couple of times. But, to tell the truth, I don't think he has the brains to be a dangerous plotter. A dangerous plotter hardly ever bulges a muscle at you before he's ready to make his move."

"Look, will you allow the Fenians have chapters all over this country?"

"Sure. There's Irishmen everywhere."

"All right. You, my boy, and those other deputies were

drugged in widely separate places. You were likely sold those doctored smokes by some innocent Irish tobacco dealer. God knows who slipped sweets laced with henbane to my kid, but it couldn't have been the same person as poisoned *you,* right?"

"Hmm. That do add up to a spread-out organization, don't it?"

"It does. And who's better organized than the Fenian Society?"

Longarm shrugged and said, "Oh, the Klan, the Know-Nothing Party, the Women's Christian Temperance Union. But let's go along with your notion the Fenians are out to get you, Marshal. If that's the case, how come you're still alive?"

"Say again?"

"You're sitting right there breathing. How come, if O'Carroll and all your other deputies are plotting against you in the Gaelic? I know I'd hesitate to murder Billy Vail on my own. But if all the deputies in the Denver office was in with me, or even Henry who plays the typewriter out front, it'd be a snap. I'd just gun old Billy in his swivel chair, Henry and me would agree it was the deed of a person or persons unknown, and that would be that. We wouldn't have to drug total strangers, or even a member of Billy's family. We'd just do him in. But then what? You see, Marshal, an employee hardly ever murders his boss without a reason."

"Aw, them micks from the old country don't think like you and me. The reason England still *has* Ireland is that every Irishman wants to be the chief and nobody wants to be an Indian. I tell you, that punk, O'Carroll, is after my job!"

Longarm sighed and said, "I noticed. But if he had a whole Irish secret society working with him behind your back, he'd *have* it by now. He wouldn't even have to gun you and get his countrymen to swear it was me who done it. He'd only have to ask his confederate, Judge O'Hara, to fire you and appoint him to fill your place."

"Jesus, you sure paint a pretty picture, Longarm."

"I meant to. You're talking dumb, no offense. I'll go along with Irishmen sticking together. Everyone else does. But I can't buy 'em ganging up on you serious. So let's get back to whatever crime you suspicioned in connection with this fool shooting contest."

"Oh, I forgot to tell you. Half the board of directors running Amalgamated Ammo have Irish names!"

"Christ, Marshal, everybody has to have *some* damn sort of name! I've double-checked what Vail already told me about Amalgamated. I even asked the Denver *Post* to look into the trust and wire me about 'em. The only crime I can pin on them is the paid assassination of ducks and, to tell the truth, they ain't even very good at that."

"Doesn't their front man, Slade, have a record?"

"He does. For mail fraud, not armed robbery. And I don't think Slade's an Irish name. I don't buy a Fenian plot, and the shootoff, dumb as it might be, don't read as a deep, dark anything. I'll tell you true, I've already wired Denver I'm ready to come home. For there ain't a thing going on in these parts that calls for all the fuss you've made."

Moran's voice got curiously soft as he said, "Then you're against me, too. I might have known."

"Marshal, nobody's against you. You got five whole deputies here to work out mayhaps a little skullduggery involving a possible land grab and the murder of one old crazy woman, so—"

Then Moran was on his feet, saying mean things about Longarm's mother as he went for his sidearm!

Longarm kicked his feet out from under the man before he could draw his old Patterson Conversion and only had to pistol-whip once before he had Moran flat on his face with his hands cuffed behind him. As the older man chewed the dirt and sobbed Longarm climbed off him, saying gently, "We'd best take you to your field office by way of this back alley, Marshal. It wouldn't do for the townees to see us arresting one another."

As he hauled Moran to his feet the older man sobbed, "You can't arrest me! I outrank you, damn your eyes!"

Longarm frog-marched Moran along the dark alley. It only took a few minutes to sneak him into the back of the Western Union. For once, things went right and O'Carroll was on duty. The young Irishman gasped. "Faith, it's Himself, and handcuffed like a desperate criminal! I hope ye have a damned foin explanation for this, Longarm!"

Longarm said, "I do. He just tried to draw on me. The marshal ain't himself this evening, Sean."

O'Carroll looked unconvinced and Longarm could have been in a sticky spot had not Moran spat, "I might have known Long was an Irish name as well! You're all in on it together, ain't you, you unwashed mother-loving micks!"

O'Carroll rose to his feet grimly. Longarm soothed, "He never meant that about your mother personal, Sean. As you can see, he's sort of confused about me, too."

As Moran raved on, O'Carroll made the Sign of the Cross and said, "Confused? Sure, the poor man's mad as a hatter! What are we to do with him, Longarm?"

"I thought you'd never ask. He's your superior. So you're the one who gets to wire Judge O'Hara for further instructions. He'd know better than me what's to be done with a lunatic working for his federal district."

"Jasus, Mary and Joseph, I'm not in too well with O'Hara. I thought him and Moran was best friends!"

"Well, right now the marshal needs all the friends he can get to help him. A doc might be able to do something about his delusions of persecution. I've done all I can. So he's all yourn."

O'Carroll moved to the back door and bawled out for his fellow deputies as Longarm sat the raving Moran down. When he wouldn't stay put, they cuffed him to the chair. As Deputy Ryan joined them Longarm told O'Carroll, "Here's the key to this set. I'd be obliged if you'd swap me cuffs and another key, just in case I get lucky again."

Chapter 12

Sylvia Norris seemed less glad to see him than he'd hoped, considering the nice things she'd said about him that morning. He found the redhead fully dressed and packing her bags. She invited him in and even kissed him, but then she said, "I have to catch the next train out, darling. The room's paid for to the end of the week, if that was what you were worried about."

"I wasn't worried about where to spend the night," he lied, "as much as I was who I'd spend it with. What's up, Red?"

"Not tonight, alas. I'm sorry, dear. I was hoping I'd be gone before you came. I hate goodbyes, don't you?"

"Yeah. You still ain't said why you ain't interested in bird watching, either, now."

She dimpled and asked, "What birds? The perishing swamp's a bloody disaster. The area's been poisoned by acidic ground water. The few species who can live under such wretched conditions are all well known. The Royal Society would hardly publish a paper on the common mosquito or the Norwegian rat. So I'm off."

"I noticed. What's the hurry?"

"Train schedule. If I don't catch the next one I'll be stuck here all night, and . . . Oh, Custis, I didn't mean that the way it might have *sounded*. I'm really very fond of you, but . . ."

He smiled crookedly and said, "I'm usually the one stuck for words at times like these, Red. Don't worry, I won't cry. I know the feeling when it's time to just be getting on down the road. Need help getting your bags to the depot?"

She said he was a doll for being so understanding and that she had already arranged for someone to load her aboard the train. Longarm didn't ask what he looked like. He asked her for the key to the room.

She gave it to him, but said, "You'd better wait until I leave before you have a word with the desk downstairs. Possession is nine points when a hotel's as crowded as this one, you know."

He said he'd noticed that and stole a friendly feel as he asked if she had to leave right away. She sighed and said she did. So he let go of her, even though he wondered why she was in such a hurry to catch a train that wouldn't be leaving for at least an hour, if he'd read the timetable right. If they weren't to be lovers any more, he wanted her out of there, too. The evening was still young, and she'd been right about hotel rooms being hard to get in Tangleroost.

He kissed her *adios*, to be a good sport, and that was the end of Sylvia, he hoped.

After she had left the room to him, he sat on the bed to have a smoke and make sure nobody tried to take the room away from him when the train did arrive. An hour later he heard the train pull in. So when someone knocked on the door he got back up to defend his territory.

142

But it wasn't the room clerk looking for an argument. It was O'Carroll. The deputy was out of breath. He said, "They're holding me train, so I can't say much. We're taking Himself home. Judge O'Hara feels it's best, since he's suspected for some time the old man was getting dotty."

"That makes sense. Who are you leaving in charge here?"

O'Carroll looked blank. "Nobody. There's nothing here for the federal government to worry about, Longarm. Poor Moran was just after making mountains out of molehills."

"Sure, but there ought to be *some* damned lawman here, at least until the contest is over."

In the distance a train whistle sounded impatiently. "I'm off," said O'Carroll. "You do what you like. Good hunting, Longarm."

Longarm called after him, "Come back here, damn it! I ain't even with the Arkansas office!" But O'Carroll paid him no mind. So, when Longarm got tired of talking to an empty hallway, he shut the door and sat down again, cursing fit to bust.

Then he had to laugh. A good night's rest wouldn't hurt him, even if he had to spend it alone. In the morning he would wire home again, and not even Billy Vail could expect a Colorado lawman to defend an Arkansas swamp against . . . what?

He decided not to worry about it. There were crooks all over creation, and a man could only eat off one plate at a time. What happened in Arkansas was no business of Colorado. The only thing he was still a mite angry about was that henbane someone had got him to smoke. That was the only thing about poor old Moran's wild notions that still held water, sort of. But, hell, there were

143

a lot of things he didn't know and likely never would.

He finished a safer cheroot and was fixing to go down and talk to the room clerk when there came another tapping on his chamber door. This one was so gentle it was sneaky and a male voice whispered, "Are you in there, darling?"

Longarm snuffed the lamp, got up, and cracked the door open shyly.

The Smithsonian dude sporting the deer-stalker cap was grinning in at him like a lovesick fool. "Thank heavens!" he whispered. "They told me you were leaving on that train just now!"

Longarm reached out, grabbed a fist full of shirt, and hauled him inside, saying, "They told you true."

Then he threw the dude on the bed and told him to stay put as he struck a match to light the lamp. The frightened young gent on the bed gasped, "Don't hurt me! If it's money you want I . . . Say, aren't you that sheriff I met yesterday?"

"Close enough," Longarm said. "The redhead's left for greener pastures. If it's any consolation, she walked out on me, too. Ain't women fickle?"

The dude sat up, looking less frightened. "Well, in that case we don't have much to talk about, right?" he said.

"Wrong. I ain't interested in which of us she liked better. I got more serious questions to ask. You can start by giving me your name again."

"I'm Wilbur Croft. As you know, I'm with the Smithsonian."

"Doing what? Are you a professor, or do I just call you doc?"

"Neither. I'm an assistant to Dr. Kramer, the chemist

of our team. If it's any business of your's."

"I think it might be. I told Sylvia I wouldn't tell on her and now I can't. But, while friendly rivalry may be one thing, it's a dirty bird as shits in its own nest."

"I don't know what you're talking about, Longarm."

"You don't? I do. The redhead just left to go home and write a paper or something on the Tangleroost. She just said the swamp's polluted with acid water. Who do you reckon told her?"

"How should I know? No doubt she tested the local water."

"With what? I just watched her pack. I didn't see no chemistry set. The redhead was lazy. Why bother doing things the hard way when you can steal field notes or get other folks' findings for a little fun? She screwed me to find out what I might know, too. That was fair. I enjoy that kind of questioning myself. This very day Tess Winslow carried a vial of swamp water back to your camp for testing. You saved the Royal Society some work by telling Sylvia what your own lab workers found. I'll allow she was great in bed, but would you say that was *ethical,* Croft?"

"I suppose you have some proof to go with your wild accusations?"

Longarm shook his head. "Nope. Don't need none. I ain't about to arrest a grown man on such a childish charge. But if I was to mention even what you *might* have done to the Smithsonian Institute, you'd sure have some serious discussion with your boss, and I'd say the odds on you keeping your job would be about fifty–fifty, wouldn't you?"

Croft looked sick as he said, "All right. What do you want from me? Money?"

145

"I probably make at least as much as an assistant bird watcher. But you *are* going to give me some scientific assistance, ain't you?"

"What do you want to know? I don't think anyone on the Smithsonian team is up to anything dishonest, Sheriff."

"I know. *You're* the rotten apple in *that* barrel. But you got more book-learning than me, and you know about research and such. So I'm sending you up to Pine Bluff to do me some of the same."

"Don't be ridiculous! I can't leave the expedition!"

"Sure you can. There's a train in the morning. If you want to get laid in the meantime, I know two horny sisters who'll screw you silly tonight. But you'll have to make your own excuses for a few days off in Pine Bluff. I don't lie as good as you."

The next day went sort of tedious for Longarm. Billy Vail had sent a night letter telling him he could come on home if it was all right with his old pard, Marshal Moran. The coroner's jury found, after some deliberation, that the Grannywitch had been killed by a person or persons unknown. Such things, they said, were always happening to niggers anyway. They tabled Longarm's suggestions that the woman had been a breed and that they really should be thinking about appointing another local police force. Parson Moore opined that any heathen living alone in a swamp who wasn't white counted as a nigger in *his* Good Book, and Swanson said by the time they could advertise for a new set of lawmen the contest would be over, so what the hell.

Young Wilbur Croft had no trouble excusing himself from the Smithsonian camp for a few days. They probably thought he was coming down with something when he limped in after spending a night with the Halifax girls.

As Longarm saw him off he said the sisters had asked about him as well. Longarm told him just to get on up to the big city and let him worry about the local wildlife for now.

The others who went out in the swamp that day had better luck this time. A big flock of awfully dumb geese flew in and, before they could figure out that there wasn't much to eat in the Tangleroost, most of them had been joyously shot dead. So Slade didn't look as ridiculous that night when he wrote out a handsome check to Sweet Sioux. The hitherto morose breed said he was going back to Deadwood, where a man could spend money sensible. Calamity Jane allowed she would tag along to help. Longarm saw them off with mixed emotions. For, though old Calamity was a pest, she'd backed him good one time in the Black Hills, and Sweet Sioux was even better with a gun. Longarm had nobody else to turn to if someone in Arkansas decided to get frisky.

Nobody did that night, and before the night was over he was tempted to pay the Halifax sisters another visit. But he decided to pass. The trouble with womankind was that it never seemed to rain but it poured. Either Luke or Lester, alone, made sense for a man with a hotel bed at his disposal. He doubted the management of the hotel would let him get away with a slam-bang screaming orgy. They had raised enough of a fuss before they had decided it made more sense to let him keep the redhead's room than to fight him for it.

So, on the third day he rose, well rested and suffering from loneliness. He might have slept later had not so many guns been going off since dawn.

He went down to breakfast and asked the waitress about the noise. She said all the other guests were already out in the Tangleroost and added, "Passengers."

He grimaced and said he would have eggs with his steak anyway. The swamp was downwind from the dining room. He was half finished when Jason Slade came in, rubbing his eyes, to ask if someone had declared war. Longarm invited the representative to join him and told him, "You won't look as dumb this evening. Passengers coming in and, once they start, they just keep coming. There may be dumber critters with wings, but if there are, I've never seen 'em."

"I thought you said the Smithsonian people told you the Tangleroost had been spoiled for bird shooting, Longarm."

"Passengers don't count as birds. They think they're locusts. Or they would if anything that dumb could think. Eat a good breakfast. By noon the stink will ruin your appetite for days."

Slade grinned. "Hot damn! That's more like it. I don't mind telling you, my company was vexed by the first two days of our contest. How many head do you reckon the winner will bring in tonight?"

"Hell, Slade, you don't count passengers by the head. You weigh 'em by the ton. You'd best borrow some freight scales off the railroad for the judging. If it's a big flock, the boys will bring in hundreds without bothering to shoot 'em. If you're really lazy, you don't even have to *club* passengers. They stomp each other unconscious, all trying to roost on one limb. Like I said, dumb. They like to crowd up, even when there's room."

Jason ordered flapjacks, then said he had heard the passengers were declining in numbers since the old days, when they'd been known to fly over all day in one big cloud. Longarm shrugged and said, "The flocks ain't as famous as they was before the War. But don't worry. You never see a *small* flock of passengers. They can't

148

seem to fly unless it's a total stampede. Don't ask me why. By this time tomorrow they'll have flown on, total. You never see one or a dozen passengers. They're like women. Either none at all or too many to handle."

He decided not to have pie with breakfast and leaned back to drink coffee and smoke instead. Slade gulped his food as if he wanted to go watch the parade. Longarm knew better. But he knew he'd go, anyway. It was sort of the way you felt about a fire engine going by—you just had to watch.

They went up on the railroad bank to do so. Tess Winslow and the other Smithsonian folk were already up there, watching the dark sky over the Tangleroost. It looked more like a gathering storm than a flock of birds. Slade said, "My God, there must be millions of them!"

Longarm had already told him that, so he didn't answer. Tess sobbed, "Oh, Custis, make them stop!"

He frowned down at her, wondering if Moran's lunacy was catching. Then he saw that she meant the hunters, not the birds, when a punt gun blasted straight up to blow an awesome hole in the cloud of birds. It didn't last long. Other fool pigeons filled in the gap while the hundred or so nailed by the punt were still falling. Tess said, "The poor birds are confused and exhausted. They don't know whether to roost or fly on, so they're just circling and circling. Oh, there goes another hundred at least!"

"Volley of ten-gauge, I'd say," nodded Longarm. "It's just as well they ain't ready to roost yet, Tess. Soon as they get closer to them guns, you'll *really* see feathers fly!"

"It's inhuman," said one of the men from the bird-watching committee.

Longarm couldn't argue that. The birds were no brighter than grasshoppers, and the idiots shooting up

149

into them weren't too human, either. Even Slade looked a mite disgusted as he told Longarm, "You were right. We *will* have to weigh the downed pigeons by the ton tonight. You'd think they'd have the sense to fly away! What's holding them over those woods, Longarm?"

"The woods, of course," Longarm said. "This flyway used to be solid woods, from the gulf to way up in Canada. Now the treetops are just sort of islands spread out amid farmland. Passengers don't light on anything that doesn't look like a tree. I know, because the flock that ruined our orchard one time never set a dainty foot on a fencepost, our house, and such."

Tess was staring at him, wide-eyed. He smiled and said, "I hope I ain't upsetting you, some way. I told you before about the time I met up with passengers, Miss Tess."

"That's it!" she said. "It's so obvious, once you think about it! You've put your finger on what's wiping out the passenger pigeon!"

He blinked and stared up at the swirling dark sky. "Do them fool birds look extinct to you right now, girl?" he asked her.

"No, but don't you see? They may be, all too soon, if mankind continues to clear the hardwoods from the bottomlands all over their natural range. The panic settlers report isn't the natural behavior of the species. Ever since Boone came through the Cumberland gap we've been cutting down their *trees,* poor things!"

He nodded, but said, "I reckon you'll find most bottomlands is owned by humans now, Miss Tess. I can see how this may dismay a bird who don't like to stroll on the ground, but you can't grow much corn in a hardwood forest."

"That's true. And, unlike crows or sparrows, passen-

150

ger pigeons don't eat corn. Their natural food is forest mast. Mostly beechnuts."

"They're in trouble, then. Most farmers clear beech first. They think it poisons the soil. Don't know if that's true, but I know what they cut." He took a drag on his cheroot. "Ain't no kind of nuts growing over in that dead forest, anyhow. Tell me something, Miss Tess. If someone was to spread lots of lime on that swamp, then drain it, would the soil spring back to life?"

She said, "Of course. Oh, I meant to tell you. That water sample I took the other day assayed as mild sulfuric acid with traces of lead. We think the water may be boiling up through an underground lode of galena. That's a sulfur-lead ore."

"I know what galena is," he said. "They mine galena all over the Ozarks. Is the lead in the water worth digging for?"

She shook her head. "No. There's not even enough heavy metal to harm the soil. It's the sulfuric acid that's doing the real damage. Why do you ask?"

He shrugged. "I'm paid to ask dumb questions. I've got rid of a mess of puzzle pieces, but there's still some left. I got to go send some more wires. So I'll see you later, hear?"

He walked off along the track. Tess followed him out of earshot of the others before she asked him, "Custis, have you been avoiding me?"

"Not working hard at it. Why do you ask, Miss Tess?"

"When did I become *Miss* Tess? Are you angry at me, for some reason?"

He said, "Not hardly," but didn't explain further. Some women were like that. They'd look at a man like he was in dire need of a shave and a haircut and then, as soon as he stopped trying, come back at him all batty-eyed.

He repeated that he'd see her later and left her standing there to work it out as she saw fit. She was pretty, but his life was already confused enough.

He went to the Western Union office. The clerk told him the wires seemed to be down, for some reason. He swore and said, "I thought passengers didn't roost on telegraph wires, but I reckon we live and learn. Professor Darwin says there's always some critters who adapt to changing conditions. That's what he calls finding a place to set when there ain't no place to set—adapting. I'll come back later to see if it's been fixed. Have all them other deputies vacated your back room?"

The telegrapher said they had, and asked why. Longarm said he might want to use it as a jail, if he ever arrested anyone again. The curious clerk asked who that might be. Longarm said if he knew he'd have arrested them by now.

He went back out. He didn't want Tess to pester him again, so he headed for the saloon by way of a cinder alley running between the business block and the swamp. With everyone in town either shooting passengers or watching them get shot, the alley was naturally deserted. Or so he thought until someone pegged a shot at him from way down the block and then, having missed by yards, lit out into the trees as if he might have something on his conscience. Longarm took after the ragged-ass bastard in the wool hat and whiskers, drawing his own .44 on the run. Then he started to wonder why he'd done a fool thing like that as he jumped a fallen log, slipped on a mushy dead pigeon, and fell on his ass as a volley of shotgun blasts parted the air where his hair had just been.

Longarm cursed and muttered, "Suckered!" as he cuddled up to the mossy log and heard more buckshot thunking into it from the far side. As if that wasn't bad enough, some son of a bitch firing from the other direction blew his Stetson off with number-nine buck. He rolled over and fired at the haze of blue gunsmoke lingering in the brush that way. He heard someone yelp like a kicked cur-dog and decided that direction was his best bet, since they had him cut off from town for sure. There was no sense presenting a crawling ass as a target, so he leaped up and dove head-first into the briar canes and, sure enough, made it before a blast of buckshot swept through it after him. On the far side a ragged-ass stranger was rolling about in agony, moaning he'd been gutshot. Longarm pistol-whipped him quietly and then took off without lingering for further first aid. More buckshot and what sounded like .44-40 slugs were pacing him to either side as he zigzagged through the trees, hoping to find cover before shot and ball found him. He dove over another fallen tree, saw yet another had fallen atop it to form a V-shaped nest of punky timber, and decided this was as good a place to make a stand as any. He cursed himself for having left his Winchester at the hotel as he reloaded and waited, hoping they weren't as smart as him. He knew that if *he* had a fool pinned down in such a piss-poor place, the poor bastard would be done for.

A million years went by. Then he heard someone call out, "See him, Rafe? We cain't let him git away, now that he's seen Tom's fool face!"

Another voice called out from the other side, "Shut up and jest keep looking. He cain't have gone fur."

Longarm knew there had to be more than two. That first volley had added up to at least half a dozen trigger-happy rascals. So when he spied one passing the open end of his hide, he held his fire. The unkempt bastard figured to pass without looking his way.

But it just wasn't to be. At the last minute the wool-hatted shotgunner turned, as if to call out to somebody, and as their eyes met and his jaw dropped, Longarm fired. You didn't mess with a man pointing a double-barreled ten-gauge at you.

Chapter 13

The shotgunner went down, of course. But that made someone Longarm couldn't see yell, "Ahint them timbers! I sees his gunsmoke!"

Longarm hunkered down as more shot and ball commenced to chew hell out of his half-ass fort. The hell of it was that with all the other guns going off more innocent all around, Longarm knew that nobody on his side was likely to even wonder who was shooting so much this close to town. On the other hand, he was too far from town to try for a running fight. They simply had him, if they knew their business.

It sounded like they might. Someone yelled, "Hold your fire! Here's what we'd best do, boys. Let's all reload and, on my command, rush the rascal from all sides at once. He ain't got but a sixgun, and nobody has eyes in the back of his head!"

A follower of more mortal clay, bless him, called out sort of plaintively, "What about the poor bastards coming in the way he *can* see, Rafe?"

Rafe called back, "Them's the breaks. He cain't git

all of us, and them as goes is going for a good cause. Is everyone loaded up?"

They seemed to be, and Longarm wasn't cheered by the numbers as they called the roll in a circle all around him. He got his back as far as it would go into the V. He didn't know what good that would do when someone popped over the back of it, but a man had to do something at a time like this. He wondered what the last man down at the Little Bighorn had done. He sure knew now how the poor bastard must have *felt!*

He heard a sudden rustle in the air and the sound of breaking twigs all around. He tensed, assuming it was an all-out charge. Then, as pigeon shit rained down on him, he saw that the flock, or a good part of it, had just gotten too tired to keep flying. The birds sure added up to total confusion when enough of them landed all at once, or tried to.

There wasn't room enough in any one tree, but the passengers tried anyway, so a whole mess of them came down in a bunch when their weight broke the rotten limb they had chosen. As the air filled with a blizzard of feathers and bird shit, Longarm made his own unexpected move. He leaped up and took off, firing at such dim targets as he could make out in the fluttering chaos. He downed at least one of them, and then he was alone in the woods save for millions of fool birds trying to fan his hair and shit in it all at once. By the time he'd staggered out of the pigeon blizzard he was back in the alley. Seeing the back door of the saloon ahead, he charged in through the kitchen, surprising the hell out of a Chinese cook and a whore having coffee. He ran out to the main room, backed into a corner, and told the assembled crowd he'd had just about enough of this shit.

Another painted gal seated on the bar laughed and

said, "You sure have, honey! Where did you just crawl from, a chicken coop?"

He grinned sheepishly. "I wish. All right, I can see by your duds that none of you other gents was with me in the swamp just now. Do any of you want to be deputies of a deputy? I got to go back and see what I wrought. Got to get my hat back, too."

There were no takers at first. Then a couple of townees said they would back his play, if only he'd tell them what the hell it was. He did and they said they would follow if he went first. He said that was fair enough.

By the time he'd gotten his Winchester and led his small posse back into the Tangleroost, the passengers had decided to roost in other parts. They'd flown on, save for the dead ones that seemed to get crushed every time they landed.

He found his Stetson first. It was damaged more by pigeon shit than buckshot. He put it on and moved toward the sticker brush to find the man he'd gutshot was still there, but not moaning any more. One of the townees stared soberly down at the corpse and said, "I know this rascal. He's one of Parson Moore's Holy Rollers!"

Longarm said, "No, he ain't. I checked out the Church of Eternal Salvation, and it ain't Holy Roller. It's a some-what more confused cult."

He peered about, got his bearings from the first body, and moved deeper into the Tangleroost. One of his followers balked and said, "They're still shooting at you up ahead, Longarm!"

"Them's the bird killers, you idjet," another townee snorted. "They's at least a mile off now, chasing birds." Then he spat and added, "Hope they all get sucked under by quicksand. Things was a lot more calm and peacable afore they come."

Another man grumbled, "Easy for *you* to say. You got a steady job with the railroad. I hardly cut enough hair to matter these days."

Longarm spotted a pair of dirty bare feet ahead, told the others to spread out and cover him, and moved in for a look-see. He saw that it was the one he'd downed from the V of the fallen trees ahead. The ten-gauge lay in the muck nearby. He called the others in and asked if anyone knew this rascal. The barber opined that he sure could have used a shave and a haircut. A railroader spat and said, "I don't know his name, but he's one of them Holy Whatevers, too. I used to see the whole bunch passing my backyard gate on their way to roll about in some pond as used to be out yonder in the woods, when the Tangleroost was still woods. How come all them holy bearded wonders was after you, Longarm?"

"That's one of the things I mean to ask Parson Moore, if ever I catch up with him. Would you boys be good enough to look around for any others in this neck of the woods and report them to your coroner? I have to get a move on if I hope to talk to more active members of the flock."

As he headed back toward town, one of the townees took charge but said the coroner, Swanson, would be working on the railroad most of the day. Longarm yelled back to work things out as best they knew how and legged on faster.

He knew the parson lived on the far side of his church-barn at the far end of town. It was still easier walking along the trackside high ground, and cutting corners through woods full of whiskered shotgunners, even ones on your own side, could change your life forever. So Tess Winslow spotted Longarm from her higher perch on the causeway and came running after him, shouting something. He turned and waited, polite, but as she came within earshot he said, "You'd best go back to your camp and stay there for now. I just learned the birds ain't the only ones in possible danger at the moment."

She ran up and wrapped her arms about him, sobbing, "I just heard! Oh, Custis, what if they'd killed you?" Then she sniffed and added, "Good heavens, what have you got all over you, and *me*, I fear?"

He chuckled and said, "That's a dumb question for a bird watcher to ask. Don't almost-extinct pigeons stink? Look on the bright side. You get to go home and clean up now. I can't. I got to discuss religion with Parson Moore, and you can't tag along, for he seems to take it mighty serious."

She stepped away, brushing her tan whipcord with her hand and then thinking better of it as she saw what she got on her hand. "The parson's not home," she said. "I saw him just a few minutes ago from up on the tracks."

"Do tell. Which way was he headed Tess?"

She pointed. "West, as fast as he could get his buckboard team to travel. There were some other men with him. They looked like trash whites."

"They might not have been that decent," said Longarm as he scanned his mental map of the area. Then he shrugged. "Maybe a light wagon can forge to the higher ground up the riverside, if the driver knows what he's doing. I'd still best have a look at the old skunk's quarters."

"I'm coming with you," she announced, reaching down to unbutton her skirt and get out her garter gun. He started to object. Then he shrugged and said, "Well, I know you can handle that sidearm better than most men, and I might need someone to cover me. So come on. Only be ready to hit the dirt the moment I even hint you ought to."

159

She agreed her outfit couldn't get any dirtier. So they moved on. As they passed the church he explained there was no sense examining a structure used by the whole town for secrets. He brought her up to date on his recent misadventures as they went on to the parsonage.

"Is Moore a fake preacher?" she asked. "Not exactly," he said. "His particular sect is a mish-mash of old-time religions. They started as break-away Congregationalists, stole the Book of Mormon for further inspiration, and decided the hard-shell Baptists had wallowing in creeks about right. Moore is only one of many ignorant country preachers of the new and sort of confused revelation. But it's starting to look like he's a mean one. Lord knows what he told his brethren in other parts the Lord wanted them to do. But the old gent running the tobacco stand in the Denver Union Depot will no doubt fill in some of the details when I wire my office to arrest him. Can't wire just now. Wires are down."

Tess gasped and said, "That accounts for all those others who were poisoned, too! But why on earth did Parson Moore do it?"

"He didn't. He got others to do it. He didn't ask even a heaven-bound fool to murder anyone. Notice, nobody *died* from that henbane. He told his fanatics they was only slowing us all down in the name of the Lord. Like I said, the details can wait."

"I'm not talking about *how* they tried to prevent you from ever getting here, Custis. I know how they did and, when that didn't work, how they just tried to murder you a few minutes ago. You still haven't told me *why!*"

He paused by a vine-covered picket fence to stare harder at the frame parsonage on the far side of the neatly kept yard. "I'm still working on some of that," he said. "I've know all along someone didn't want outsiders who might have brains poking about in this neck of the woods. They tried to stop the big shootoff to begin with, knowing that it would attract outsiders. When they couldn't do that, they tried at least to keep out smart cusses like me. They thought poor old Moran was smarter than he was. They didn't worry as much about the Irish greenhorns, who might think bogs is the natural state of nature. O'Carroll and his crew meant well, but they missed them hid-out outlaws entire before I got here."

She asked if the ex-outlaws who'd been acting as the local law were in cahoots with the cultists. He said, "Moore had to know 'em, since he was one of the town council as hired 'em. Cover me as I move in. You tidy up the loose strings after you unravel the main knot."

He moved across the yard as Tess trained her gun on the door and windows. The side door was unlocked, so he opened it. He heard a muffled moaning somewhere in the house. He made sure there was a round in the chamber of his Winchester before he started pushing doors open with the muzzle. In the pantry he found a bitty dark girl in a black dress on the floor, on her side, trussed like a turkey, and gagged with a dish towel.

He asked if she was alone in the house. She nodded, her big sloe eyes pleading up at him. He dropped to his haunches beside her, leaned his carbine against a cupboard, and got the gag out first as he told her, "I'm law. So lay still as I untie you. Who left you in this fix, and how come?"

She coughed lint, got her voice back, and said she was Parson Moore's housekeeper and that she had no idea why Moore and some other gents had treated her so mean just now.

He told her he could make an educated guess as he untied her wrists and ankles. By the time he had her sitting up, Tess had joined them in the pantry. Longarm told her not to point that gun at the pretty little quarterbreed and added, "You was right about Moore leaving town. It wouldn't be delicate to ask this former employee of his whether they spared her because of past additional duties or just because they didn't want to shoot off guns this close to the tracks. What's your name, girl?"

The housekeeper said her name was Rose and insisted she'd done nothing wrong, including what he might be hinting at. Longarm helped her to her feet. "All right. I want you to go to your own quarters, lock the door, and stay put till we're ready to jaw with you in further detail. You ain't under arrest, but you may be a federal witness, as soon as I figure out what federal laws them other rascals may have *broke*."

She said she lived up in the roof peak. Longarm told her to go and, when she'd done so, proceeded to search the house with Tess tagging along commenting on the furnishings as women will.

Tess said that aside from being well kept, the velvet-draped and freshly wallpapered house spelled more money than she'd thought the average preacher man got paid. Longarm said, "His ragged flock of hardscrabble farm folk never paid for that rosewood table, either. Not even when they still lived here. Most are long gone. Yet here he lingered, living mighty high on the hog. It does make one wonder. I knew he was a local big shot and a partner in the land-holding company. But, yeah, someone's been slipping him some pin money."

"Do you think he was . . . you know . . . with that girl upstairs?"

"Depends on how holy he felt about her, I reckon. She seems to have worked sort of hard at housekeeping for a play-pretty, though. I reckon she's just a pretty little breed who needed a job."

"I'd say she had some African blood as well," Tess sniffed.

He said, "I noticed. I've been wondering about that ever since I checked the notions of his sect out. The Congregationalists was one spearhead of the Abolitionist movement, along with the Quakers and other such outfits. The Book of Mormon ain't decided on colored folk, but Joseph Smith, whether you buy his notions entire or not, did admire Indians. He said they was a lost tribe of Israel."

He went to a desk, rummaged through it, and said, "Yep, here's a copy of the very book, along with a King James Bible. Yet Parson Moore dismissed the Grannywitch as a crazy old nigger in a mighty un-Christian way for a preacher man."

Tess shrugged and said, "A lot of people don't practice what they preach. Moore just tried to have you murdered, and here you are mulling over his views about colored people? Honestly, Custis, I don't understand you at all!"

He moved on as he replied, "That's likely because you've studied more birds than lawmen, Tess. It's the little things folks say that give bigger things away. Moore tried to keep me from going out to the sulfur springs by dismissing the Grannywitch they'd already killed, maybe only hours before, as an ignorant outcast who wouldn't be able to tell me much. He did call her a nigger, even though he must have known she was white and Indian. *We* call that overstating one's argument. He was trying to establish that he didn't like her and couldn't know her too well. He didn't have anything against her."

"I see what you mean. A man who really hated non-

163

whites would hardly have been sleeping with that slut upstairs."

Longarm grimaced. "Don't talk dirty about gals you don't know. We do know Moore and the Grannywitch was in cahoots before they had to gun her, knowing I'd be dropping by to see her one way or the other, sooner or later."

"My God, the parson was involved in witchcraft, too?"

"Not hardly. His sect wasn't *that* crazy. Neither was the old spey woman, most likely. An outcast living alone in the woods has to make a living somehow. So, like many of her kind, the Grannywitch must have sold moonshine, love potions, and such to the more ignorant farmer folk, before the flood. Yet, like the parson with hardly any flock, she lingered on after the flood drove her customers away. I reckon they enlisted her to guard them mysterious springs. The few locals left was already afraid of her, and she could report on any poking about them boils out there. When army engineers got too curious she poisoned 'em, after poisoning the springs to discourage 'em even more. I wired the Corps of Engineers about their survey a long time ago. They have this bottomland down as drainage-worthy but not worth the expanse because it's so polluted and malarial."

Tess frowned and followed him into the luxurious bathroom he had found, asking, "Wait a minute, Custis. I can see how that witch might have made those army men feel sick, but there's no way she could have poisoned those springs! They're *still* spewing acid water, and there's simply no way she could have done it. The whole swamp's at least as sour as vinegar, and there are thirty-odd square miles of flood to account for! It would take a tank car full of pure sulfuric acid at the very least. There's no way she could have poured *that* much in a hole in the ground."

He said he'd assumed as much as he bent over, turned a bath tap, and said, "Glory be, it's hot! There must still be some fire in the boiler by that kitchen range."

As Tess watched him filling the tub, she asked why on earth he wanted to do that. He said, "When the Lord sends golden chances my way I don't question 'em. Hadn't you noticed I'm covered head to toe with passenger poop?"

She gave a startled laugh. "So am I. But you can't take a bath *here!*"

"Sure I can. Old Moore ain't likely to come back, and even if he does there's a lock on this room's door. I don't know about you, but I mean to enjoy a good hot soak. Care to join me?"

She gasped and backed half out the door. He asked her to get in or get out, as he meant to lock the door before he stripped. She crawfished all the way out. But as he approached to lock it in her face Tess asked, sort of red-faced, "Why don't you ask that maid in the attic to come down and scrub your back, you brute?"

He said, "You know, that ain't a bad idea. Why don't you go on home and take your own bath?"

She said, "The water's cold in camp." Then she started to unbutton her bodice as she stepped back in and let him close the door behind her. "I suppose it will be all right if I keep my slip on, at least. Do you promise you'll behave?"

He said he sure would, leaned his Winchester in the corner, and proceeded to undress, saying, "Once we give our duds time to dry, we can shake the pigeon dust off the surface. It's the juice coming through as leaves the real stink on one's hide."

She stepped demurely out of her whipcord habit and hung it on a doorhook before she turned around in her chemise, gasped, and said, "Oh, you shouldn't have taken *everything* off!"

Longarm didn't reply until he'd lowered his more private parts out of sight in the warm water. Then he said, "What you can't see can't hurt you, and my underpants would take forever to dry. Come on in. The water's fine."

She hesitated, then moved closer to the big tub, asking if he was certain she could trust him to behave like a gentleman. He said he hardly ever behaved like a lady, in or out of a bathtub. She giggled and got in, easing down into the water with her back to him and her hips between his spread legs. He reached for soap and a string washrag and proceeded to lather her back as well as he could. Then he said, "Slip that fool chemise off so we can do this right."

"Oh, I couldn't. You'd see me naked!"

When he pointed out her tail was under soapy water and her tits was aimed the other way, she demurely agreed it wouldn't hurt to pull off the now soggy chemise and fold it neatly over the edge of the tub. She also agreed it felt grand, as she put it, when he got to scrubbing her naked hide for her right. As they got more used to bathing together like old pals, Tess relaxed and didn't object too loud when he hauled her back closer to rub the front of her down as well. She must have felt what was pressing against her tailbone as he soaped her firm, slippery breasts, but she didn't let on she was enjoying more than an innocent bath until he had a wet hand down between her thighs, parting her wet pubic thatch.

She gasped, "Oh, Custis! You promised to behave right!" But she didn't try to cross her legs as he stroked her wet clit faster, asking if that was what she meant. She bit her lower lip and hissed, "Watch those damned nails! Oh, I'm never going to be able to face you again, now that you've taken such liberties with me!"

"You don't have to face me. But I sure wish you'd raise up a little. The rest of me is feeling sort of left out."

She giggled like a kid telling dirty stories and said, "You idiot, it wouldn't work that way."

"How do you know? Have you ever tried it this way?"

"Never mind how I know. I just know, damn it, and . . . Oooh, could you move those fingers just a little faster, dear?"

He could and he did, and in the end Tess was willing to show him what couldn't be done by raising her naked buttocks from the bottom of the tub and sliding them up against him until, suddenly, they discovered it could be.

As his wet shaft entered her Tess sobbed, "Oh, you're touching me!"

"You just noticed?"

"I didn't mean with your *hand*, you brute. Lots of girls let a boy friend feel a . . . well . . . free sample. But you shouldn't be going all the way with me, unless, of course, we're engaged?"

He growled, "Honey, do you want to screw, or do you want to talk dumb? I can't do both at once. Not as good, anyways."

She sobbed that he was just awful and commenced to bounce on his turgid shaft with both hands helping his wrist as he strummed her old banjo at the same time. She naturally came ahead of him and started crying about the way he'd just used and abused her. He decided since she was never going to talk to him they might as well say goodbye right. So as she came a second time, all soapy on the bath mat with a roll of towels under her tailbone to protect it as he pounded her, Tess agreed she might talk to him some more, at the hotel, where they'd have all night to do this nicer.

Chapter 14

Coroner Swanson announced the jury would meet at the church as usual, once a night train went through and the section could close down for a spell. Meanwhile, Jason Slade was having his own problems as he and his judges, some of whom were also to weigh evidence for the coroner later, tried to figure out who had shot the most passenger pigeons that day.

Some in the crowd made surly remarks about not aiming to be cheated this time. Slade was trying not to, as far as Longarm could tell. Not even Longarm could count every beak in a waist-high pile of dead pigeons covered with blood and dung. He gave up and went to see if the wire was up yet. It wasn't, so he tried the dispatch office by the water tower. Swanson said the railroad's line was still operating, since a railroad couldn't operate without one. He said it was against regulations to patch private messages through to Western Union lines farther out and added that, though *he* was willing to take the chance, the other railroad men they would have to go through might snitch and cost him his job. Longarm lit a smoke and said, "Try her this way. Wire for instructions on a surly federal agent pestering you to get a message through to his home office. That way they're sure to wire back, asking what the hell I want. Then you tell them to tell Denver I've about wrapped up my case and I'm ready to haul ass. You might add that, if they don't, I don't care *who* robs their infernal trains from here on."

"Jesus, are you expecting a train robbery, too, Longarm? I heard about Moore going loco, but I can't see him robbing trains!"

"He's more likely to be hopping freights between now and the time we catch up with him. I'll tell you all about his dastardly deeds at the meeting tonight. No sense telling the same tale over and over to the same coroner."

Swanson agreed, and they shook on it. Back at the saloon, Longarm discovered that the Halifax sisters, of all unexpected contest entrants, had won the grand prize that night. Luke and Lester didn't spot him in the crowd, and they looked so proud that it would have been mean of him to mention that he'd last seen the two dozen ducks atop their awesome pile of pigeons some time back, in their smokehouse. He ducked out before they could invite him home with them. A man who believed in quality more than quantity had other plans for later that evening. Tess had said she could hardly wait to try it on a softer pillow.

He was standing out front, enjoying a moonlight smoke, when yet another female voice hissed at him sneaky. He moved down to see Rose, the parson's housemaid, lurking in the shadows. She said she'd been keeping an eye on the parsonage from the empty house next door, like he'd told her to, but that nobody had come back and she was getting spooked. Everyone knew there

170

were haunts in the Tangleroost at night.

He said, "What some may have seen for spooks was more likely men working under cover of darkness, Rose. Men up to sneaky stuff hardly ever answer when folk call out to 'em. They just tend to fade away, spooky, see?"

"I'm still scared. You can arrest me if you like. But I ain't about to spend a night alone out there in the trees with the hoot owls!"

"You ain't under arrest. Like I told you before, you're a friendly witness, and I'm still deputizing you to watch that parsonage, at least until after the coroner's meeting in a little while. I don't think anyone's likely to come back. If they do, you're to run to the church and tell me. After the meeting I'll fetch you myself and see that you have a place to stay here in town. A pretty gal like you won't have trouble finding a job now, for I suspicion this town is about to enjoy a land boom."

She started to object. He shushed her and sent her back to her post with a friendly pat on the behind. For such a short gal, she had nicer padding down there than he had expected.

A little while later another train came in. It was a freight—passenger combo and, from the numbers leaping off as it stopped, he could see word of the passengers had somehow gotten about.

He shook his head in disgust. Tess had just said, in a calmer moment, that they might not see another bird for days to come. Passengers scared hell out of everything, including themselves. The scientists suspicioned that was why they flew in such numbers or not at all. All the fuss and feathers shook up natural bird-eaters, so they only managed to grab crumbs out of the flock as the others bred safely in the center. Tess said passengers might not be able to breed like other birds, away from the madding crowd. He had suspected all along that she knew a lot about breeding.

He blinked when he heard a gunshot up along the tracks somewhere. It was a hell of a time and place to be potting pigeons. Some of the others in the crowd paused to look about. Then they shrugged and moved on as Longarm walked against the current.

Deputy Sean O'Carroll spotted him about the same time in the confusion. As they stopped and shook by the railroad bank, Longarm asked if he was a full marshal yet and, if so, what brought him back to Tangleroost.

The young Irishman swore darkly and said, "That thraitor to his race, Judge O'Hara, appointed another Yank he said was more experienced to be after replacing Moran. Moran's in the hospital at Pine Bluff, as ye might have guessed. I was just sent back to find out why the telegraph wire seems to be down, and what it might mean to the law."

Longarm nodded. "I figure someone cut it, too. I have been sending wires all over the country, and it might have made someone nervous. Did you hear a pistol shot just now? Sounded like it came from the far side of that train."

O'Carroll said he'd heard what could have been a shot but hadn't considered it important in such noisy surroundings.

"The hunt's over for the night. We'd best have a look," Longarm said.

Parson Moore was sprawled down the far side of the embankment, his head under the black scummy water ponded higher on that side. Longarm would have known that rusty suit anywhere. He hauled the body out by its

172

high-button shoes just to make sure.

"He doubled back to catch a train out. I didn't think that wagon trace went anywhere important. He sure was a sneaky old gent. But someone sneakier just shot him, as you see. Now all we got to do is figure out who."

"Don't we start with why, Longarm?" O'Carroll asked.

"Hell, the why's no mystery. A silent partner knew I was fixing to arrest him on sight. So he was killed to keep him from discussing the case further with me, and ...Damn, there goes the infernal train! Oh, well, the conductor wouldn't be able to tell us the names of every-one who just got off, in any case. Let's go tell the coroner he's got another cause of death to decide. He's running these yards when he ain't the coroner."

But when they walked down to the water tower, the dispatcher on duty told them Swanson had left a short spell back because he had to put on his Sunday suit for the hearing in the church.

Longarm told O'Carroll, "You'd best stick with me, then. You need experience, Irish, and this meeting might be interesting."

He filled O'Carroll in on all the goings-on since he and the other deputies had left. O'Carroll whistled. "You do lead an active life, me bucko. They was waiting for the chance to get you alone, eh?"

"They'd have had to try for me soon, anyway. No offense, but poor old Moran had the rest of you just running around in circles after his own mad suspicions. In a way it was lucky, though. For had not at least one outside lawman taken some interest in this jerk-water stretch of nothing much, they'd have likely pulled it off. They discouraged the only other federal men who ever even looked at the place, and who knows when any of us would have been back?"

173

"Moran was sure something crooked was going on. But, now, would you mind telling what in the divvil it *was*, Longarm?"

Longarm pointed at the ghostly loom of whitewashed siding ahead and said, "We're almost there, and it's tedious to tell the same tale twice. Listen tight as I tell it to the coroner's jury, and I'll only have to say things once."

They went in. Swanson and some of the others were there. The railroading coroner said others were still due, since they had to replace Parson Moore and another normally present member. He was one of the bodies tonight's panel was meeting to discuss.

Longarm found some folding chairs for himself and O'Carroll. By the time they were set up and smoking comfortably, the others had filed in and Swanson called the jury to order.

Longarm faced the long table and made short work of the dead and accounted for, tossing in the parson who had led or ordered the attack in the woods. "It ain't for me to tell you gents your business," he said, "but anyone can see most everyone who died around here recent was either shot lawsome or murdered by them I shot."

Coroner Swanson said that sounded sensible and announced, "The findings of this jury are that the late Parson Moore and his Holy Rollers was up to something awful and got caught by the law. Do I hear any objections?"

Down at the end of the table the livery man, Thorp, said, "Yeah, me. I can't see how the parson wound up shot by the law if these two lawman say it wasn't them as shot him."

"We still don't know what on earth the parson and his

followers was up to," another juror said. "Do *you* know, Longarm?"

Longarm nodded. "I can make an educated guess. I sent someone up to Pine Bluff to check out my suspicions, and I'll be able to prove things better when he gets back with survey maps, old records, and such," he told them.

"Hell, Longarm, we know how smart you are. Go ahead and *guess!*"

There was a murmur of agreement. So Longarm complied. "Starting in the sweet by and by, this township, as you all know, was fertile bottomland, fit for logging and corn save for the few times a year it got flooded. Generally the water dried up within a week or so after the Arkansas topped the levee. So folks could make at least a living. Folk who're making a living on land don't sell it cheap. The parson and his pals wanted it cheap."

A prissy old gent in gold-rimmed specs gasped and said, "Hold on! I'm a shareholder in the land-holding company! Are you calling me a crook?"

"Don't get your bowels in an uproar," Longarm said. "I never said *everyone* who chipped into the parson's scheme knew the full facts. Most of you, I'm sure, did it as a possible investment and out of pure charity to the flooded-out farmers. So those who acted in good faith are about to wind up richer than they went in."

"That's more like it!" grinned Swanson. "Keep talking. I like what you're saying about *money,* Longarm."

Longarm nodded. "Figured you might. All right. You all know about them boils near the cabin of the Grannywitch, where water had never boiled under the levee before. A big mistake the crooks behind the whole plot made was lacing that water with acid. It did discourage

175

them army engineers and it did play hell with the land it flooded, making it seem even more worthless. But the first thing any outsider with the brains of a gnat might question was how come Arkansas river water was boiling acid when the river lay below the level of the swamp in any case. The Arkansas runs a mite alkali, if anything."

Swanson nodded and said, "Of course! The Grannywitch was out there poisoning them springs as she scared the curious away!"

"They ain't springs," said Longarm flatly. "Someone laid a pipeline clean across three miles or more of woodland into what was only ponds, before kids noticed so many haunts in the woods out there at night."

"My God!" gasped Swanson. "Who could have done us so dirty, and where do they get that acid water from, it if ain't natural?"

Longarm said, "That's easy. This is naturally wet country and, like I mentioned before, there ain't no culverts in the railroad causeway. So rainwater ponds behind what amounts to a six-mile-long dam. A pipeline running from the uphill side of the tracks to the made-up sulfur springs keeps them boiling even when it ain't rained all that recently. As to the who, would you mind keeping your hands on the table where a man can see 'em, Coroner Swanson?"

Swanson slid his chair back from the table, his hands still out of sight. So Longarm had no choice but to blow him over backwards with the derringer he'd been holding palmed against such a sudden emergency. As everyone else sprang up, young O'Carroll got his own gun out and roared, "Don't none of yez move!"

Longarm told O'Carroll not to shoot anybody else as he walked over to see how Swanson was making out on the far side of the table. The railroading coroner was either dead or in the habit of staring at rafters with two smoking holes in his breastbone, mighty blank-faced.

Longarm said, "That was sure dumb. All I had on him was circumstantial."

"How did you know it was him at all?" asked Thorp.

The one in glasses said, "Don't talk stupid. Didn't you see Swanson go for his own guns, first?"

"That wasn't what made me suspicion him," Longarm said. "I figured it out by a process of elimination. That's what we call it when we wind up with nobody left. I failed to see how a barber, a livery man, or even a blacksmith could have managed so much sheer engineering. It had to be a man with the know-how to run a whole railroad section. They don't give such jobs to idjets. Yet a kid who made mud pies with any imagination could have told the railroad they needed some drainage culverts between high ground and low. *He* told *me* he'd suggested it and that the head office had said no. I knew right off he had to be lying, unless the railroad was run by fools. He was also the only one who could have laid hands on so much pipe without the rest of you noticing. As mayor, he was the only one who could have made sure the law here in town wouldn't take the reports of haunts in the woods seriously."

Thorp said, "By gum, it *was* Swanson who hired them gents you real lawmen said was crooks!"

Gold-rims told Thorp to shut up and let Longarm finish. "He was able to furnish the tools and the skills," Longarm said. "Parson Moore furnished dumb, fanatic manpower. Anyone who noticed work along the track, filling in old culverts and such, would hardly question work they assumed was Swanson's regular business. I reckon they just laid the pipe through a drain hole left by more innocent engineers, then filled it in to feed them

177

boils out in the ever-growing swamp."

"What about the acid?" asked O'Carroll.

Longarm said, "That added up to sneaky railroading, too. You see, every telegraph set along the line has batteries filled with lead plates and sulfuric acid. It's a chore to get rid of used-up battery acid, since folks do fuss when you pour it over their back fence. I feel sure he made arrangements to let the railroad dump acid on the far side of his section. They'd have no reason to ask why he was being so good to them. Like I said, it's a chore to get rid of such wastes. If it's any comfort, a few carloads of slaked lime through them same pipes ought to sweeten the whole swamp before you just cap the pipeline and let it dry some. It's up to the railroad and the army engineers whether they want to do more serious ditching around here. Since you innocents will be in charge here now, the political bullshit's up to you. Who's the coroner now?"

The one with gold-rimmed glasses said, "I nominate me. I finished school, damn it." Nobody argued the point.

In the end, they dragged Swanson out of the way, held another meeting, and decided Longarm deserved a vote of confidence as well.

He held up a hand for silence. "Hold on. Before this all winds up wrong in the Arkansas papers, I want Deputy O'Carroll here to get the credit for this case."

O'Carroll looked more surprised than anyone else there. He told Longarm, "You can't be serious, man! What have I ever done for ye to deserve such a grand favor?"

Longarm said, "You ain't done it yet. The paperwork you'll be stuck with figures to be a bitch, but you said you had ambition."

"I do indeed. But how can you give credit for your case away?"

"Easy. I ain't as ambitious as you. I don't want old Billy Vail's swivel chair. It's made him fat and grumpy. So you and these gents work the rest out as you see fit. I got better places to be right now."

Chapter 15

Back at the house across from the parsonage, little Rose leaped up on Longarm like a scared pup when she saw it was him instead of a haunt who'd joined her in the darkness. He patted her soft back to calm her as he soothed, "There, there; it's all over, little gal. Parson Moore ain't never coming back. Since the last time we spoke, he turned up dead. Do you know of any living kin he might have had?"

She said, "No, he was a widower. And, despite what that white gal said, I don't think he wanted to start up again with any woman. He just seemed interested in money. He had a lot of it in a little tin box. But I don't think it's there now."

Longarm said he didn't think so either, but that they'd best have a look. As they went over to the parsonage, Rose said she'd been thinking about where she might stay now, and that she had a sister living on the far side of town. She asked if she still had to stay at the hotel.

He said, "It would be a mite crowded. I'll see you safely to your kin, once we give the parsonage one last look."

They did. Rose showed him secret drawers and such he might have never noticed. But Moore had lit out with his little tin box and it was up to O'Carroll, now, to find out where Swanson might have cached it.

As they finished going through some bedroom drawers the house-proud housekeeper sighed wistfully at the bed she'd made herself that morning and said, "I wish I'd known in time. I turned the heavy mattress and put fresh linens on that bed, all for nothing!"

Her words were innocent enough. But, as she met Longarm's gaze steadily with her big sloe eyes, he could well believe that neither the parson nor any other man had helped her to wrinkle bed linens of late.

He felt as sure, from the way her perky breasts were heaving, that it might not have been her own notion.

He hauled her in as he suggested, "It'd be a shame to let all that effort go to waste. We got plenty of time to mess that bed back the way it was, you know."

She hugged him back, but asked, "You promise you won't tell my older sister? She put me to work here, she said, to keep me out of trouble. She said working for a parson might cure my warm nature."

They were across the bed and Longarm had her skirts up around her tawny hips to calm her down. As he entered her, Rose gasped and said, "Oh, Lord, that's just the cure the doctor ordered. But can't we take our clothes off, darling?"

He laughed and said, "Sure we can. They ain't nailed on. We might even have time for a friendly bath before we have to put 'em on again. I can't catch a train out this side of sunrise . . . oops, I meant midnight."

Rose was too excited by then to catch the slip, judging from the way she was moving under him. He knew he really should be saving some of his strength for Tess,

181

who was waiting for him at the hotel. By now she would surely have heard about the noisy meeting of the local coroner's jury, the whole town being so local. But surely a lawman was required to wind up a few last details before a case could be considered closed. Still, he knew he'd best get back to Tess this side of midnight, if he didn't want her fussing at him.

But, somehow, it was hard to keep track of the time when Rose served him coffee and cake in bed a spell later and then coyly suggested another kind of dessert. That in turn led to a messed-up bed indeed. They got coffee and cake crumbs all over themselves in the process. But Rose said she was sure the bath water was hot by now. So they ran a tub, got in together, and, Rose being Rose, wound up with more soapy water on the floor than in the tub.

He'd left his watch in the bedroom, figuring his gun rig and a naked, giggling gal were enough to carry into the bath. But he knew he was stretching his luck by the time they had finished on the same damp bath mat. He knew he deserved to be whipped with snakes for being such a rascal, but he also knew most other men would have had trouble resisting the temptation.

But all good things must come to an end, if a man knows what's good for him. So when Rose made a worried remark about her older sister being ready for bed by now, he gallantly grabbed at the chance to get them both dried off and dressed. When he did get a chance to consult his watch, he saw that he really didn't have time to escort Rose clean across town and still get back to Tess before it was too late to explain. But it would have been downright skunk-hearted to send the poor little girl home alone in the dark. So he did what a gent had to do, and she likely thought he was just being thoughtful of her sister when he walked her faster than her shorter legs were made to work. It still seemed like her infernal kin lived a hundred miles from the parsonage.

In point of fact, it only took about ten minutes to get there, and he knew he could move even faster on his own the other way.

Then Rose grabbed hold of him by her sister's garden gate and hugged him like a pretty little bear, sobbing, "Oh, darling, I still want you! Do you want me some more?"

He could tell by the tingle that he sure wanted somebody, which was surprising. He kissed her, and when they came up for air he told her gently that her notion of a stand-up moonlit screw was just too risky for her reputation. She sighed and said, "I'd invite you in, but I fear my sister would suspicion I've been wicked again, even if we acted proper in her parlor."

He said he understood, kissed her some more, and then took off before she could suggest anything else.

He chuckled sheepishly as he made it to the main street and strode innocently down it toward the hotel. He was in the clear now, even if Tess was gazing out the window of the room where he'd told her to wait for him. He could already see the front of the hotel up ahead and there was his window, gaping dark. Tess had likely gone to bed already.

As he passed the Western Union, the telegrapher who knew him stuck a head out to say the wires were back up if he wanted to send them messages, now. Longarm thanked him but said it hardly mattered at this late date. He didn't take the time to add that Swanson's cutting the Western Union line while leaving his own railroad wire up had been another dead giveaway. The case was closed, and Tess was waiting. He would have a whole night and mayhaps until noon before the Denver office got around to wondering why he wasn't on his way back. He would figure out how to say adios to the Smithsonian gal when he had to.

He entered the hotel, took the stairs up two at a time, and had to rap gently on his hired door, since he'd given Tess the key.

There was no answer. He frowned and tried the knob with one hand as he drew his .44 with the other. The door was unlocked, but as he busted in to cover the made-up bed and open closet he saw that both were empty.

He shut the door before lighting the lamp by the bed. That was when he saw the neatly folded sheets of familiar notepaper on a pillow he'd been planning to shove under something prettier right about now. He holstered his gun and unfolded the note. As he'd hoped, it wasn't a ransom note.

Tess had worded it a heap fancier, and it was almost as long as the report Billy Vail would likely still want, no matter who got the final credit for the recent confusion. But the guts of her message was that she felt just awful and wanted to say she was pure sorry for raising any false hopes when they'd been "swept away," as she called screwing.

She said she had to get away before she "gave in to forbidden desires" some more, because she was engaged to some professor back in Washington, who could be biting off more than one man could chew, in Longarm's opinion.

But what really annoyed him was the part about her leaving on the next train out no matter which way it was going. For that meant she'd been boarding the very same train O'Carroll had got down from! So all the time he'd been rushing with Rose, Tess had been long gone, blast her fickle ass, and all his sacrifices had been in vain.

He started to reach for his pocketwatch. Then he smiled in a wistful way and decided that, whatever time it was, it was still too late. A man was supposed to snatch at the gold rings as the merry-go-round of life swung him past them, and he wasn't sure he was up to starting from scratch with two gals right now, even if both of them were willing.

He unrolled his possibles to get out the Maryland rye a man had to pack in case of snakebite or other emergencies. He pulled the cork with his teeth and poured himself a stiff nightcap. Then he raised the hotel tumbler to the lonesome-looking bed and said, "Here's looking at you, Tess, even if you ain't there. If we never see you *or* your passenger pigeons again, we'll just have to somehow get along without you."

Watch for

LONGARM IN THE HARD ROCK COUNTRY

eighty-sixth novel in the bold
LONGARM series from Jove

coming in February!